A BRIDE FOR JASON

Ace reporter Jason Edwards wants to marry Carly Smith, but Carly is a career girl and their families have been feuding for years. When she takes a job with Jason's family her aim is to safeguard her livelihood by exposing their unsavoury dealings. But Jason's instincts compel him to question her motives. Will the truth allow him to overcome the obstacles and still make Carly his bride? And when Carly discovers his reasons for doubting her, can she forgive him?

BEVERLEY WINTER

◆

A BRIDE FOR JASON

Complete and Unabridged

LINFORD
Leicester

First published in Great Britain in 2006

First Linford Edition
published 2007

Copyright © 2006 by Beverley Winter

British Library CIP Data

Winter, Beverley
  A bride for Jason.—Large print ed.—
  Linford romance library
  1. Love stories
  2. Large type books
  I. Title
  823.9'2 [F]

  ISBN 978–1–84617–909–9

Published by
F. A. Thorpe (Publishing)
Anstey, Leicestershire

Set by Words & Graphics Ltd.
Anstey, Leicestershire
Printed and bound in Great Britain by
T. J. International Ltd., Padstow, Cornwall

This book is printed on acid-free paper

1

Jason Edwards, ace reporter for The Natal News, rubbed his bloodshot eyes as he reached for the telephone on his desk. His voice came out in a hoarse, protesting croak. 'Edwards.'

Sweet heaven, but he was tired! More tired than he could remember ever since arriving on God's green earth some three decades ago. Even his voice box had got up and gone to Johannesburg. He had to face it, he'd burned up all his rocket fuel. Big Time.

'To my office,' a voice barked in his ear. 'Now!'

Jason shoved one hand over the receiver and uttered something short and sharp. He was in no mood for another summons from his editor-in-chief. He'd only just arrived back in the country, for pity's sake! Did the man never sleep? It was past ten on a

Sunday night. Even the gulls who constantly skimmed over the nearby Indian Ocean had given up and gone to bed.

Jason cleared his throat. 'I'm on my way, sir,' he clipped.

On his way to where? Another beastly assignment in another troubled part of the globe, probably. He'd just jetted in from the Philippines and before that it had been Iraq. He'd stared death in the face once or twice in the last fortnight and it hadn't been a pleasant experience. However, he'd lived to tell the tale. Anyone would think he was now entitled to a few hours' sleep.

'I want this story investigated, and I want it done yesterday,' James O'Brien growled before he'd even sat down. 'I won't have that fool at the Natal Mercury getting there before us. I intend to run the story next week.'

He glared at his best investigative journalist over the top of his heavy spectacles in a manner which suggested that Jason was personally responsible for all the ills of the world.

He flung a buff-coloured folder across the desk.

'My source tells me these people are vicious, so watch it. They'll do anything to protect their little racket. I advise you to go undercover if you want to save your skin.'

Reluctantly Jason reached for the file. 'No problem.'

He was used to dangerous assignments, but now was as good a time as any to face the truth — he was becoming fed up with the whole business. He'd just reached his thirtieth birthday and what did he have to show for it? No family, no social life, no settled abode. Nothing but work. He didn't even own a dog.

Life, he reflected soberly, was a dreary round of hurriedly-packed suitcases, depressing hotel rooms and strange, unpalatable food. And each time he returned to Durban he was forced to placate his irritating landlady with some gift or other to keep her sweet. It was driving him nuts.

The woman couldn't understand why he was never there, and only last week had informed him she would prefer to let his room to a *real* lodger. What she meant was a wimp of a man she could control, and Jason Edwards was a man who wouldn't be controlled . . . least of all by some dominating female with a frustrated maternal instinct. Nothing annoyed him more than a woman who felt the need to mother him.

He scowled at the folder without seeing it. 'I'll get on to it.'

Apart from his less than satisfactory private life and the fact that his career no longer appeared to hold any challenges, Jason had to admit that he was lonely. Lonely, bored and burnt out. It wasn't that he needed a change of scene, either; with his kind of lifestyle he was forced to endure a change of scene just about every week.

His gaze sharpened as he forced himself to read the words pencilled hurriedly on the outside of the file.

Illegal immigrants from Mozambique? He looked up incredulously. 'What kind of an assignment is this?'

He was used to covering world events, for crying out loud! The last thing he wanted at this low point in his life was a meaningless visit out into the sticks. Anyway, it would only serve to remind him of his grandfather and the constant guilt which had begun to nag at the back of his mind.

James O'Brien reached for a cigar from the carved wooden box on his desk and sniffed it.

'Oh, it'll be tougher than it looks, Edwards. There's a fraudulent little scheme going on in Northern Zululand, with illegals coming into South Africa from over the border at an alarming rate. Filthy place, Northern Zululand. Full of swamps and malaria. And where there are swamps there'll be mosquitoes.'

He sniffed the cigar once more before lighting it. 'If you don't take the required medication with you, be it on your own head. Ever been up there before?'

Jason ignored the heavy thumping which had begun to pummel his chest. 'I'm familiar with the area.'

'Good.'

With careless disregard, his boss inhaled a lungful and blew the unpleasant result into Jason's face before offering a further explanation.

'It appears that any foreigner, providing he meets certain criteria, may gain access in the country, no questions asked. He simply crosses the border into the Kosi Game Reserve and if he's not eaten by lions en route he hops over the fence and makes for a certain farm in the area. What could be easier? Especially when the farmer in question is prepared to hide him while he lies low.'

'Surely the police should be handling this?'

'Oh, they've been investigating, all right. No results, which is hardly surprising.'

'What criteria?'

'Huh? Oh . . . that will be for you to find out, won't it? Most of these illegals are poor so it couldn't be money they're offering in exchange for free passage, yet by all accounts this farmer is making a killing. All rumours at this point, of course.'

Jason's head snapped up. The hair on the back of his neck had risen, a sure sign that his journalistic instincts hadn't gone to sleep after all.

'Which farmer?'

'It's all there in the file. I want the full story by next weekend or you're dead meat.'

Jason looked thoughtful. His grandfather's farm happened to be situated near the Kosi Game Reserve, which was rather convenient. He'd ease his conscience by paying the old fellow that long overdue visit and sniff out the immigrant situation from there.

He stood up. 'I'll do my best.'

Jason opened the folder and glanced at the single sheet it contained. There did not appear to be much to go on. As he read, his grey eyes narrowed in sudden shock.

'Kosi Park . . . '

James O'Brien stared. 'You know the place?'

A bland mask fell over Jason's features. 'I've been there.'

What the dickens was his grandfather up to? Everybody knew that Jasper Campbell was a law unto himself; a feisty old man who'd made as many enemies as he had friends over the years. But he wasn't dishonest. He'd never stepped outside the law before, so why would he start now? Surely the old man couldn't be that hard up for cash?

He said firmly, 'There must be some mistake. I know the owner of this farm personally. He would never condone anything like this.'

'No mistake, Edwards. Those are the facts. All you have to do is verify them.'

'Whose facts?'

'I never divulge my source.'

'Your source could be wrong. This

man wouldn't allow his property to be used as an illegal gateway into the country, and certainly not for any financial gain. No way.'

The other man gave a cynical laugh. 'You'll find that greed corrupts even the best of us. Your loyalty is touching, but I doubt you'll be able to save the man's lily-white reputation. It might interest you know that one of the immigrants was caught recently, and he sang like a lark.'

He added with relish, 'He was rescued from a gory death by a warden in the Kosi Game Reserve and was so 'grateful' that he spilled the beans ... or some of them, in a garbled fashion. I'm certain this is no wild goose chase, Jason. In fact, it's my belief this Jasper Campbell is in it up to his eyeballs.'

He inhaled another lungful. 'I intend to publish, and I don't care who gets wrecked in the process.'

Jason's grey eyes darkened to pewter. Deliberately wrecking lives in the so-called interests of a good story was his boss's usual modus operandi, and a genuine desire to elicit the truth had very little to do with it. For some reason, this no longer amused him.

'I won't need a cover,' he said firmly.

He'd go as Jason Edwards, long-lost grandson, returning to the fold. Like the Prodigal, come to his senses!

It would be good to get his life into gear and shoulder his family responsibilities. He realised belatedly that he'd never been the kind of man who enjoyed living entirely for himself. He needed a family to protect and defend, so he'd do what he should have done years ago, he'd settle down and become a bona fide son of the soil.

He'd find himself a wife, build her a homestead and sire a gaggle of barefooted, free-spirited farm children who wouldn't even know what a newspaper looked like!

Now that the decision was made he felt like a bird let loose from its cage. It was a pity his mother wasn't alive to witness the spectacle.

James O'Brien was regarding him in blatant irritation. 'Don't stand there grinning, Edwards. Get on with it.'

Jason cleared his throat. 'There is something I must say, first. This will be my last assignment for The Natal News.'

'What do you mean, your last . . . ?'

'I'm leaving the paper,' Jason repeated clearly. 'I quit. My resignation will be in the post this evening.'

The editor's jaw appeared to have become unhinged. His mouth flapped open and shut like that of a dying mackerel.

'Don't be a fool, Edwards! You have a brilliant career ahead of you . . . I've had my eye on you for promotion. Have you lost one of your two brain cells, man?'

'No, sir. Actually, it's the sanest decision I've ever made.'

'And when did you make this *sane* decision?'

'In the last few minutes.'

The editor shook his head in disgust. 'If you're contemplating joining the opposition, I'll wring your stinking neck.'

'No need, sir. I won't be working for another paper at all. I'll be doing something completely different.'

'Like what?'

Jason's eyes gleamed. 'Farming. It has always been my grandfather's wish that I take over the family farm,' he explained. 'He's almost eighty and it's time I accepted the assignment.'

He paused for breath. 'And just where, may I ask, is this most irresistible of family farms?'

Jason hid a grin. He said deliberately, 'It's in Northern Zululand. It adjoins the Kosi Game Reserve.'

There was a stunned silence, during which the editor of The Natal News made a supreme effort to recover himself. 'I see. In that case,' he snapped, 'you'll have no difficulty in finding this Campbell fellow and exposing the whole can of worms.'

Jason reached for the door handle. 'None at all,' he concurred politely. 'Goodnight, sir.'

He drove to the small airport north of Durban where he kept his cherished blue and white single-engined aircraft.

Not many people were about at this hour. He parked in his usual place behind the hangar and handed the keys of his blue Ford Fiesta to the pop-eyed young mechanic who had served him faithfully over the years.

'The car's all yours, Sean. Where I'm going, I'll have no need of it.'

'Honest? Gee, thanks, Mister Edwards,' the youth stammered.

'Pleasure's mine,' Jason assured him. He was glad to be able to help the guy. In future he'd be using one of his grandfather's numerous vehicles. As he remembered, there was a silver Mercedes and a green Land Rover amongst them, and either would suit his needs.

'I'll be keeping the plane up north for a while,' he told the mechanic casually before stowing his two small suitcases and making his way to the office to file a flight plan.

Ignoring the upsurge of excitement in the pit of his stomach, Jason went through the pre-flight check with his usual meticulous care. As the plane lifted effortlessly into the night sky, his firm, well-shaped mouth curved into a grin.

'Face it, Edwards,' he admonished himself happily as the lights of Durban receded into the distance, 'you've chewed off the bark; now let's see you getting down to the wood!'

★   ★   ★

Carly Smith stared about her in shocked amazement. To say that Jasper Campbell's farm was rundown was the understatement of the year. So much for all that Campbell pride she'd heard so much about!

The fences needed repairing, the old, magnificent farmhouse had seen better days and everything in sight looked as though it could do with a coat of paint, especially the wooden pillars supporting the wide, shady veranda. They were probably so rotten they'd collapse on her even before she reached the front door! And as for the roof tiles . . . well, even if she did land the job she wouldn't be required to actually sleep under them, thank goodness. She'd be commuting to work every day in her little red Mini.

Sudden doubts filled her mind. Perhaps she should reconsider . . . ?

'No, Carly,' she admonished herself firmly, 'you've come too far to chicken out now . . . certainly not because of a few rotten beams which look as though they might fall down at the first stiff wind which comes along.'

She wasn't going to relinquish her dreams just because the property of a prospective employer didn't quite measure up to her high standards. Determinedly she climbed out of the Mini and marched up the veranda steps to the solid-looking oak door. Before she could lift a hand to the knocker an elderly voice sounded from one end of the veranda.

'Miss Smith?'

Carly spun around. The old man sitting in a worn blue armchair, his knees covered with a woollen rug despite the mounting heat, was regarding her unsmilingly from shrewd blue eyes.

With an effort he stood up and looked her over; a tall, stooped giant of a man with a thatch of white hair which matched his neatly trimmed beard. If the beard had been a little longer, the stomach a little larger and the cheeks a little rounder, he'd have been Santa Claus.

'You'll be Miss Carlotta Smith,' he stated, offering one blue-veined hand.

Carly smiled warmly as she took it, and then gulped. Blimey, he might look like a fragile bag of bones, but his handshake was enough to crush her fingers!

'Good morning,' she responded politely.

'Yes, I'm Carly Smith, and I have an appointment to see Mr Jasper Campbell at ten-thirty.'

'You're early. Sit down,' the old man commanded, gesturing towards a painted wicker chair. Carly did as she was told. The dear old thing was obviously lonely, and there'd be no harm in giving him a little of her company. As he'd pointed out, she was early.

A tray of tea was waiting on the round table beside it. Being a kind-hearted girl, she gave him another smile and asked, 'Shall I pour your tea?'

It seemed to be the most natural thing in the world. 'I always pour for Gran and Grandpa,' she explained in a motherly voice, and picked up the teapot.

At first the old man looked a little taken aback, and then hid a smile.

'And what about one of these lovely scones?'

The poor dear looked as though he could do with a good square meal. 'They're wholemeal,' she noted happily.

'With strawberry jam and fresh, farm cream; so very nourishing.'

His mouth twitched. 'Thank you.'

Carly gave a sigh of pure pleasure as she handed him a plate. 'The scones look as light as air. Crisp on the outside, too. Someone in this household is a very good cook.'

He inclined his head. 'My housekeeper, Joyce Thembisa.'

'I'm afraid baking is not one of my skills,' Carly confided sadly. 'I do try, but it's no use, really, so I leave all that to my grandmother. I prefer to be out in the pastures, seeing to the cows.'

He looked up quickly. 'You do?'

'Oh, definitely. I've always loved cows. They have such lovely brown eyes.'

Carly's own eyes, equally brown and lovely, smiled into his. 'It may sound odd to you, but I even love their smell . . . all sort of warm and grassy.'

There were two cups on the tray and she was dying of thirst, but Carly wouldn't have dreamed of helping

18

herself uninvited. Instead, she commented on the weather and the state of this year's maize crop and then glanced at her watch.

'It's been lovely chatting to you, Mr, er . . . sir, but I'd best be getting to my interview now, if you don't mind. I shouldn't like to keep Mr Campbell waiting. I expect he's inside the house?'

She rose and straightened the pencil slim black skirt she'd worn in an effort to appear mature and businesslike. After all, she'd be running a large dairy herd if she was successful at this interview.

'Enjoy the rest of your morning, sir,' she offered politely. 'Goodbye.'

The man's eyes gleamed with amusement. 'You'll do,' he said with satisfaction.

'I beg your pardon?'

He waved her back into the chair. 'The job's yours if you want it, Miss Smith.' He indicated the teapot, 'and the other cup's for you, lass. I'm delighted to find a young woman with good manners and a kindly regard for others. Help yourself. There's plenty in the pot.'

Carly shook her head. 'You don't understand. I'm here for an interview with a Mister Jasper Campbell.'

'I am Jasper Campbell.'

Carly's pink mouth fell open. She hadn't expected this old, almost-Santa to be the boss she'd hoped to work for. He didn't look fit enough to stand let alone run a farm this size.

'You . . . you are?' she gasped.

He became businesslike. 'I'd like to offer you the position you applied for, Miss Smith. You may start work tomorrow morning at five o'clock sharp.'

'But . . . you haven't even looked at my CV. I have it here . . . '

Not that there was much in it to recommend her. At twenty-two years of age she still had almost no work experience to speak of. To please her grandfather she'd taken that wretched typing course after she'd left school only to find that secretarial jobs bored her to tears. After that she'd persuaded Grandpa to send her to Cedara Agricultural College to study farming, which was what she'd wanted to do in the first place. If she hadn't tried so hard to please her grandparents, Carly reflected ruefully, she wouldn't have wasted all this time in getting started.

Jasper Campbell ignored her protests. 'No need for a CV, I'm a good judge of character. Your letter said you've been trained at Cedara, which is good enough for me. Besides,' the blue eyes held a decided twinkle, 'you like cows, and so do I. You'll take charge of my dairy herd, Miss Smith, but the beef herd is run by my manager, Rodney Mason.' He sighed softly, ' . . . or what's left of it.'

'Thank you, I should like that.'

'There will be a one month's trial period during which time you'll be answerable to Mr Mason, and if he approves of your work you will be offered a permanent contract. As to salary . . . ' he named a figure which was more than satisfactory.

Carly's mouth curved into a grin of pure delight. She'd successfully landed her first real farming job, and the fact that the position had been promised her by the man her grandfather detested, did little to dim her euphoria.

She drove home to the neighbouring farm, Jozini Acres, and accelerated up the long, dusty drive. But as her grandparents' homestead came into view her smile disappeared.

'Naturally you won't like it, Grandpa,' she muttered under her breath. When he heard what she'd done he'd be mad enough to eat bees. What she wouldn't tell him, though, was the reason she'd purposefully answered that particular advertisement in the last *Farmers' Weekly* magazine; that in order to protect her grandfather's interests she needed to know precisely what his sworn enemy was up to.

Carly's smooth brow creased into a frown. It was all rather disconcerting. She'd been fully prepared to dislike

Jasper Campbell on sight, but now that she'd actually met him she couldn't help liking him.

'Within the week,' she promised herself firmly as the Mini roared towards the house, 'I will have sussed out exactly what is going on at Kosi Park.'

2

The truth was, she was becoming heartily sick of all the undercurrent and innuendo amongst the farm labourers. She doubted her grandfather was aware of it, but there had been strange rumours abounding amongst the African wardens in the nearby game reserve as well as amongst the staff on the surrounding farms. She'd caught snatches of conversation which had disturbed her, and a lot of it concerned Kosi Park.

Despite these problems, Carly intended to make a brilliant success of her new job. Perhaps then her grandfather would dispense with his old-fashioned, chauvinistic ideas and allow her to work at home instead.

In her excitement, Carly stamped a little too hard on the accelerator so that the Mini was forced to swerve drunkenly between the potholes as it roared along in a cloud of red dust.

Daniel MacDonald, sipping his aperitif on the veranda, sighed into his glass. He and his dear wife, Mary, had tried their best to raise their orphaned granddaughter correctly, but he feared they had not made a very good job of it. Carly, despite her caring nature, was as tomboyish as ever, and still much too headstrong.

There was simply no need to churn up the drive like a ravenous warthog searching for food! When would Carlotta learn to behave like a young lady?

'Grandpa,' Carly yelled as she ran up the veranda steps, 'I have some news for you.'

It was the end of his working day and her grandfather was tired. Not that he was able to do much these days; most of the work was delegated to the labourers by the efficient foreman, Joseph Xulu. Nevertheless, it irked him that Jozini Acres was a shadow of its former self. Cattle ranching was hot, tiring work, which needed a strong, energetic, innovative man at the helm. Sadly, he was no longer able to be that man.

Something else worried him. All was not well with his Zulu workforce, a group of men who had always been loyal and hardworking. Recently they had become sullen, speaking amongst themselves in whispers. He wished he knew what it was all about.

Pushing aside his worries, he smiled indulgently at the enthusiastic light in Carly's brown eyes. Her blonde hair had come loose from its ponytail, fanning cheeks which were pink with excitement. She was the light of his life, if she but knew it, and his spirits always lifted when she was around.

Carly plonked herself down on a cane chair and poured a glass of orange juice from the jug which Trifina, their Zulu housekeeper, had left on the glass-topped table.

She drank deeply before putting down her glass. It was time to press her grandfather's buttons. 'Where's Gran? I have some news for the two of you.'

'I'm here, darling.' Mary MacDonald emerged from the doorway and smiled. 'What is it, love?'

Carly sprang up to pour her grandmother a drink, suppressing her impatience, and when the old lady was comfortably seated she wasted no further time in making her announcement.

'I've found a job,' she stated baldly. 'I'm staring work in the morning.'

Her grandfather's indulgent air fell off like tender beef from the bone. 'A job? There's no need, Carly,' he snapped. 'How many times do I have to say it? A woman's place is in the home.'

Carly rolled her eyes heavenwards. 'Grandpa, this is the twenty-first century. Women are now working outside the home, and well you know it!'

'That may be so, but I will not have you doing likewise. Are you not happy here?'

'Yes and no.'

'What kind of an answer is that?'

'Well, Grandpa dear, you know that I love this place dearly, and I've done my best to please you and be a lady. I can cook — at least, passably — and I can knit a scarf without much trouble and I can sew on a button, and do all those things a woman is traditionally supposed to do, just as Gran has taught me.'

She looked him straight in the eye. 'But you also know that I much prefer farming. I can't help it, it's in my blood, just like it's in yours. The fact that I'm a woman makes no difference at all. I want to put into practice all the new methods I've learned at Cedara and if I can't do that here then I will have to move on to where my skills will be used and appreciated. It's as simple as that.'

Her grandfather's face was thunderous. 'Dear heaven, you still have that extraordinary bee in your bonnet!'

'Yes, Grandpa, and it will never go away. I know you only agreed to send me to an agricultural college in the hope that I'd grow tired of the idea of farming and opt for some other course afterwards . . . something more lady-like, but that is not going to happen.'

'Farming is a man's job. If you are that set on farming, why not marry a farmer? It's time you settled down, my dear. Try to socialise a little more . . . go into Jozini and meet people. There are plenty of fine young men in the town.'

He paused. 'Whatever happened to that lad, Grant Mason, who was hanging around a few months ago? And Dennis Forbes, before that?'

'I told them to get lost,' Carly said forthrightly.

'Why?'

'Well, they both wanted to marry me, so what else could I do? I'm not interested in getting married, Grandpa. I don't want to be a farmer's wife or anyone's wife. I want to be a farmer in my own right.'

Daniel MacDonald rose from his chair. 'I'll not listen to any more of your nonsense, Carlotta.' He grated. 'The subject is closed.'

'I'm afraid it is not closed, Grandpa. I've decided that I will take this position. I'm sorry to disappoint you, but I must do what I'm trained for.'

'What position?'

Carly stole a look at her grandmother, expecting to see disapproval on her face. She was amazed and heartened to see the old lady regarding her with something like pride.

'I've been employed to supervise a dairy herd on a . . . on a neighbouring farm. Like I said, I'm starting work tomorrow morning, on a month's trial.'

At the disappointment on her grandmother's face she added hastily, 'I'll still be living here at Jozini Acres, Gran, don't worry. I'll travel to work every morning. The hours will be long, of course.'

'Which neighbouring farm?' her grandfather asked suspiciously.

Carly swallowed. It was now or never. The sooner she said it, the sooner her grandfather would begin to accept the idea.

'Kosi Park.'

She thought the old man had eaten fire and was now spitting smoke. 'What! You have dared to do business with my enemy?' he roared. 'You have dared to go behind my back, cap in hand, like a silly girl, to ask Jasper Campbell for a handout?'

Carly took a deep breath. 'It wasn't like that,' she reasoned. 'It's no handout, Grandpa. I'll be earning every penny, and I'm determined to do a good job if only to prove to you that I can.'

She ignored the fury in his eyes and said boldly, 'I made an interesting discovery, Grandpa. Mr Campbell is not an ogre, he's a charming old man and I liked him a lot. Unfortunately he has allowed Kosi Park to run down a little, and I could see that it makes him sad. I could also see that at his age he just hasn't the energy to keep up the old standards and I don't blame him. I intend to do my best to help.'

She smiled. 'He says it will cheer him up to have a pretty young lady around the place.'

'Jasper Campbell always could sweet talk a woman. He's a rogue! Mark my words, Carlotta, you'll have nothing but trouble if you do this thing. You'll be sorry you ever had anything to do with the man.'

Unperturbed, Carly rose and kissed him on the cheek. 'It'll all turn out for the best, Grandpa, you'll see.'

'I doubt it. All I can say is that I'm exceedingly angry,' he told her icily, and stalked into the house.

'Phew,' Carly muttered. 'Round one to Carlotta. I think.'

Her grandmother smiled. 'I thought you acquitted yourself very well, my dear. It's not everyone who has the courage to stand up to Daniel.'

Carly stared at the old lady in amazement. 'I thought you'd take Grandpa's side.'

'Not always, dear. There are times

when I could shake him, like now.'

'Really?'

'Yes. He has one or two blind spots, but he's a good man, and very protective of his own, which is why he crossed swords with Jasper Campbell in the first place.'

'What happened?'

'Oh, it was a very long time ago ... something to do with a young woman they both wanted to marry. She ended up having neither of them, and each man blamed the other.

'Then there was the matter of the stock thefts and the broken fences and one or two other unfortunate things which tend to happen on a farm, and there's been bad blood between them ever since.'

She shook her head in puzzlement. 'So silly, really. They both went on to marry women they loved and to become successful farmers, so why the ongoing feud?'

She added thoughtfully, 'I'm proud of you, Carly. I can see that you are determined to be your own person, and that's good, but at the same time please be patient with your grandfather. He only wants what he believes to be the best for you. He'll see your point of view eventually, but you must give him time.'

Two dimples appeared on the lined cheeks, reminding Carly of what a beauty her grandmother once was.

'We'll not let it disturb our dinner, dear. Do take a peep into the kitchen and make sure that Trifina hasn't forgotten to whip the cream for the trifle, will you?'

Carly hurried down the passage and sniffed appreciatively at the aroma which greeted her.

'Something smells good, Trifina.'

The housekeeper turned around and put her hands on her ample hips. 'Your grandfather is as angry as a wet hornet. What have you said to upset him?' she chided with the familiarity of an old servant. 'Now he'll tell me that my roast beef has given him indigestion again.'

Carly sighed. 'He'll be angry for a few days, Trifina, and then he'll calm down.' Glad of a sympathetic ear, she explained the situation. 'I'll be out working at Kosi Park so you'll have to take over some of my chores for the next month, if you don't mind. I'll have a word with my grandmother . . . you can expect a raise in salary.'

Trifina nodded. 'You had better go to bed early, then, and I will have your breakfast ready on time.'

'What on earth . . . ?' Carly's eyes flew open in the darkness. Something had awakened her and she had no idea what it was.

Sensing her unease, the tawny Alsatian puppy lying on a rug next to the window cocked her ears and gave a soft growl.

'Hush, Amber,' Carly cautioned. She sat up and listened intently. All she could hear was the steady tick of the bedside clock and its alarm set for four o'clock.

'I must have been dreaming,' she

35

yawned, snuggling under the duvet once more. When the sound came again, she bolted upright.

It was a distant sort of drone, interspersed with hiccoughs. In a flash she was out of bed, thrusting aside her pink drapes and flinging up the old-fashioned sash window. It moved stiffly, scraping against the white-painted woodwork.

Cautiously she peered out. The pre-drawn chill stroked her cheeks, and she shivered. Just discernible were the outline of rumpled velvet hills in the distance and the dark gleam of water as the river snaked its way through the fields. A faint glow on the horizon told her the stillness of dawn would soon be exchanged for the noise of another African day.

Carly listened. The growling became louder.

'Good grief, Amber,' she gasped, 'it's an aircraft, and it's coughing its way over the pine trees near the dam. Sounds like trouble.'

A moment later she shrieked, 'it's crash landing right in the middle of Grandpa's maize!'

She watched in horrified fascination as the aircraft flopped to the earth with a loud, juddering thud and ploughed a scythe wildly through the foliage. Then the eerie, swishing sound faded into an abrupt silence.

'Grandpa,' Carly breathed in awe, 'will not be amused.'

It was the piece of land which had been used as an airstrip by the Campbells until Jasper Campbell had at one time, short of cash, been forced to sell it to her grandfather. Even the transaction had led to hostilities between the two men.

'Oh, heavens, what am I doing? Quick, Amber! There'll be someone inside the cockpit and he may be injured. We must get him out . . . '

She thrust her feet into a pair of stout shoes, flung an old anorak over her blue pyjamas and raced through the house to the front door.

A ghastly thought struck her. 'Amber, the aircraft might explode!' The glow of dawn coupled with the light of a waning moon was enough for Carly to see by as she dashed down the veranda steps and ran over the damp grass. Her grandfather's large garden gave on to the surrounding veldt where the waist-high grasses were interspersed with succulent, thorny aloes. They reared up at intervals, ghostly and robot-like in the moonlight.

When she reached the field Carly thrust aside the shoulder-length maize stalks with their fluffy golden tops and fought her way towards the plane. The foliage rustled, showering her with icy dew.

She was within twenty yards of the wreckage when something large and solid reared up out of the darkness. It clutched at her like something out of her worst nightmare, and Carly's blood froze. With what breath she still had, she opened her mouth and screamed.

3

The man was terrifyingly hard and solid and he shouldn't have been there at all. Carly's scream became a muffled squawk as two arms crushed her slim body against a hard, masculine chest.

'Little fool!' a deep voice rasped. 'What the blazes do you think you're doing? That plane could blow any minute . . . now move!'

Carly was half pulled, half pushed to the perimeter of the field and forced to the ground behind a thorn bush. 'Get down and stay there,' the voice ordered roughly.

To add to the indignity, the nightmare had flung himself on top of her and was breathing down her neck like a snorting buffalo. Amber, taking this as a signal to play, began licking their faces in a delirium of ecstasy.

'Down, you confounded animal,' the

man growled, whereupon Amber, recognising the voice of authority, subsided with a small whine.

Carly had never felt so terrified in her life. Apart from that, she was completely winded. She sucked in a lungful of air and lashed out in fury.

'Down, you confounded man,' she mimicked, 'and get your bulk off me! Your attentions are unwanted, degrading and obnoxious.'

To her relief the man immediately complied. 'Articulate as well as beautiful,' he murmured, 'nice choice of words . . . ' and rolled over with a groan. He lay on his back and remained there, heavily inert. Anyone, Carly thought acidly, would think he'd fallen asleep!

She sat up rather gingerly and then wished she hadn't. At that moment an almighty explosion rent the air, coupled with a flash of light so brilliant that it illuminated the landscape for miles around. Pieces of metal showered what was left of the crop and an acrid smell of burning filled the dawn air.

The aircraft had indeed exploded and it was a miracle they hadn't been hurt. If it hadn't been for the pilot's quick thinking in dragging her away, she might well have been killed. He'd tried to shield her with his own body, too, she realised belatedly.

Amber pressed her shivering body against Carly and gave a soft whimper. 'It's all right, love,' Carly comforted the animal.

But it was a full five minutes before she was able to heave herself unsteadily to her feet. Her legs were like cotton wool and her eyes were beginning to sting. She managed to peer through the greenery at the wreckage. It was burning steadily.

The sky brightened, revealing the full extent of the carnage. Carly's brown eyes widened. Her grandfather's field had been gouged out from one end to the other as the aircraft had scythed everything in its path. A great black pall of smoke now hung over the entire countryside and the odour was sickening.

'What will Grandpa say when he sees this lot?'

He worked hard in order to keep afloat financially, and could scarcely afford the loss of this year's profits. It was a big field and he relied heavily on the annual income from this particular crop.

Carly swallowed hard on the lump which rose in her throat. 'We'll have to rely more than ever on the cattle, Amber,' she confided, 'Grandpa will be forced to sell one or two bulls, which won't be good for the future of the herd.'

Frustration flooded her. 'Oh, if only he'd let me help. I have so many ideas . . . ' Belatedly she clapped a hand over her mouth. 'Oh, how awful of me!'

She'd been so busy thinking of their woes that she hadn't given the pilot another thought. The poor man must be in shock. 'You've had a lucky escape,' she told the inert figure awkwardly. 'I'd like to thank you for saving my life. I'm sorry I was rude, but you scared me.'

When he ignored her olive branch, she added impatiently, 'I'm Carly Smith. You've landed on our farm, Jozini Acres. Did you run out of fuel, or what? Perhaps you were heading for the farm on our eastern border, Indumeni. It's the Zulu word for 'where the thunder rolls' . . . we have a lot of storms here, you see . . . ' her voice petered out in embarrassment.

She was gabbling, but she always did that when she was nervous, and the persistent silence of this large, good-looking man was making her nervous. Even with his eyes closed he was intimidating, with that potent masculine aura and obvious physical strength.

'Perhaps you were heading for Kosi Park?' she suggested as an afterthought. 'This piece of land used to be their airstrip, but it now belongs to us. Maybe that is what confused you. No landing lights.'

Still he ignored her, and Carly frowned. She was not used to being ignored. 'Look, I'm all for letting sleeping dogs lie, but aren't you taking this a bit far?'

She leaned over and studied him curiously. He was quite gorgeous, with a straight nose, a firm, well-shaped mouth and a strong, square jaw which bore a small cleft in the middle.

Carly sighed. She was a sucker for small clefts, but not for dark stubble, and his was already showing considerably, even in the grey light. His colour didn't look too good, either.

She prodded his chest. 'Are you hurt?'

The man continued to lie on the damp earth like some pole-axed giant. As the sun peered over the hill it illuminated the patch of dried blood which had oozed from a graze on his temple. That is when it dawned on Carly that the man might actually be unconscious.

She stared at him in consternation. What now?

'I'll go for help,' she promised, ripping off her anorak and covering his chest with it before hurrying back to the house.

Trifina was busy in the kitchen, going about her early chores . . .

'Ask Joseph to bring some men,' Carly gasped, 'there's been an accident, and a man must be carried back to the house.'

She needn't have wasted her breath. Half the workforce, having heard the commotion, was already making its excited way up the hill. Carly sped back to the scene, issued instructions to two of the men, and within minutes the mud-stained, inert body had been carried into the house and installed in the guest bedroom on Mary Mac-Donald's spotless white linen.

Carly's grandparents, aroused from their bed and having watched proceedings from the shelter of the veranda, stared in perplexity at the figure on the bed.

'Poor boy,' Mary murmured as she

inspected the graze on his forehead. 'I wonder who he is?'

Carly, having hurriedly slipped into her working clothes of denim jeans and cotton shirt, peered over her grandmother's shoulder.

'Whoever he is,' she said cheerfully, hiding the sudden jerking of her pulse, 'he's bound to be in the land of nod for hours. I'm due shortly at Kosi Park to supervise the five o'clock milking, so I can't stay to find out. I'm off to have my breakfast.'

At that moment Jason Edwards opened his eyes. Instead of hurrying away, she stared in fascination. She had to admit they were stunning eyes, light grey with thick, dark lashes. They stared with total incomprehension at the concerned faces of the two elderly strangers bending over him.

For the life of him Jason Edwards couldn't work out who they were or what he was doing in their house.

'Ah. You've surfaced. I'm Mary MacDonald and this is my husband,

46

Daniel, and our granddaughter, Carly Smith. How are you feeling?'

'With my hands,' Jason quipped, attempting a smile. 'Jason Edwards. I take it I've had some sort of an accident? I don't quite remember . . . '

'Take it easy, lad. Your light aircraft landed on my property early this morning,' Daniel informed him. 'All that matters is that you're safe.'

Jason gave a groan. 'Oh, yes . . . I remember. The plane's a right-off, isn't it?'

'I'm afraid so. Where were you heading?'

'I was trying to find a landing strip somewhere around here, but it seemed to have disappeared and it was too dark to see properly so I flew out to sea while I tried to think what to do.'

He passed a hand over his aching forehead. The tight band encircling his head was no joke. He must have given his head an almighty thump.

'I flew back and circled a few times, but I'm afraid I ran out of fuel and had to put her down as best I could. I haven't been in these parts for years, but I was certain it was the right field. Did I do much damage to the crop?'

'A fair amount.'

'In that case, please accept my sincerest apologies. I will see that you are reimbursed for any losses.'

Carly fled to the kitchen. It was her big day and not even an earthquake would deter her, least of all some foolish pilot with a faulty aircraft who had robbed her grandfather of his profits. She hoped the man had insurance because her grandfather certainly hadn't.

Trifina, having served Carly her porridge followed by bacon and eggs, bustled into the guestroom with a tray. Her eyes popped as she gave Jason the once-over.

'Yes, it is as I thought.' She nodded. 'You are the grandson of old Mister Campbell from Kosi Park.'

Jason stared blearily. 'How did you know that?'

'I remember you as a boy, you were always writing things down. I used to work for your grandmother before I came here, and I knew your mother.'

She placed the tea tray on the bedside table and returned to the kitchen; happily unaware of the sudden chill she had left behind her.

'Is that correct?' Daniel demanded. 'You are Jasper Campbell's grandson?' His eyes blazed with anger. 'You're a Campbell?'

'Well, yes, but my name is Edwards, as I said. My mother was Jasper's only daughter and she married — '

'In that case,' Daniel interrupted fiercely, 'you will be on your way just as soon as it can be arranged. My driver will deliver you to your grandfather this very afternoon. I'll not extend my hospitality to a Campbell.'

Mary MacDonald looked suitably shocked. 'Over my dead body will you send the lad back today,' she declared roundly. 'I'm surprised at you, Daniel! How could you? The boy's not well

49

enough to stand, let alone be ferried around the countryside in Joseph's pick-up truck. He's to be kept quiet in bed in this very room, and that is my final word.'

It wasn't often that his gentle wife asserted her quiet authority, and Daniel had the grace to look ashamed.

'Fine, Mary,' he snapped, 'but he will go just as soon as he's well enough.'

Jason closed his eyes wearily. 'I wouldn't have believed it,' he drawled, 'but I see it's still very much alive and kicking.'

Mary picked up the teapot and began to pour the tea. 'What is?'

'The Campbell-MacDonald feud.'

Mary shot her husband a reproachful look as she passed Jason a cup. 'Yes, I suppose it is.' She sighed. 'Perhaps one day we might all grow up.'

Jason hauled himself up on to one elbow, took the cup and thanked her gratefully.

His throat felt so dry he could drink enough to lower the water level in Jozini Dam.

'We may all be of Scots origin,' he observed dryly, 'but surely we don't have to keep living in the seventeenth century?'

Daniel's head jerked up. 'What do you mean?'

Jason hid a grin. 'Naturally I'm referring to the massacre at Glencoe, when the Campbells slaughtered the MacDonalds.'

'After accepting the warmth of their hospitality for two whole weeks,' Daniel pointed out bitterly. 'The Campbells are a treacherous lot.'

Jason gulped his tea thirstily. He ignored the blinding ache in his head and decided it was time to challenge the old man's prejudices.

'On the contrary,' he argued, 'the MacDonalds were a bunch of murdering thieves and well you know it. They had it coming to them. Anyway, it was all a political thing, that massacre . . . orders from King William's cronies.'

Daniel swallowed the rest of his tea, replaced the cup on the tray with scant regard for its delicate china and marched to the door.

'You will excuse me, young man,' he flung stiffly over his shoulder, 'I have farming matters to see to.'

Jason watched his bristling departure and shook with silent laughter. 'He's as bad as my grandfather.'

Mary smiled. 'Well, that's good to know. It's awful, isn't it?' She poured him another cup of tea. 'What are we going to do about it?'

'I'll think of something, Mrs Mac-Donald.' He reached for the painkilling tablets she had so thoughtfully provided and swallowed two with his tea.

When his hostess had gone, Jason closed his eyes to think, and within minutes the answer came. He knew exactly what he would do. He would marry that delightful granddaughter of Daniel's!

She was a stunning little blonde and he remembered the feel of her as she'd cannoned into him in the early hours of that morning just before giving him the sharp, articulate edge of her tongue.

Yes, that's what he'd do! He'd make an unholy alliance with a MacDonald. Or rather, a holy one. 'That,' he stated with immense satisfaction, 'should cure those two silly old men once and for all.'

He spent the next few minutes in enthusiastic contemplation of his future bride, acknowledging wryly that his plans would in all probability not go entirely smoothly. Miss Carly Smith was bound to be as prejudiced as her grandfather, but that would not faze him. He could be as stubborn as the next man once he had made up his mind.

For the first time in months, Jason felt a new sense of purpose. Carly Smith presented just the sort of challenge he needed.

4

Carly arrived at Kosi Park just in time to see Jason Campbell's small herd of black and white cows being ushered away from the milking shed by two of the Zulu farm workers. She parked her Mini under a nearby thorn tree and frowned. Surely the animals should be going inside, not back to the pastures?

Outside the mud-stained, white-washed shed stood a row of newly-filled galvanised iron milk containers. They were obviously awaiting collection by the local milk co-operative lorry, which meant that the cows had already been milked.

Carly marched inside and did a double-take. It was the scruffiest milking parlour she'd ever seen, and horror of horrors, there were none of the usual clean, shiny milking machines she'd expected to see in operation. OK, so the farm was a bit run-down, but grief, not even one tiny machine! Did they still milk by hand?

'They're living in the dark ages here,' she muttered in disbelief. 'Who would have thought it?'

A rough, masculine voice mocked from behind. 'You must be the new milkmaid.'

Carly spun around. She looked at the tall, untidy man who had followed her into the shed and said coldly, 'I'm Carly Smith. I am here to manage Mr Campbell's dairy herd.' Milkmaid, indeed! By the look of him he was one of those hostile, hung-up men who despised women farmers. He would need to be put in his place.

'You're late,' he grunted.

'I was told to be here at five o'clock,' she pointed out. 'It's only ten to.'

'We milk at four,' he snapped.

'Since when? Mr Campbell distinctly said five.' He was one of the most disagreeable men she'd ever met. Surely he couldn't be her new boss?

She said in her best hoity-toity manner, 'And you are . . . ?'

He looked her up and down, noting with blatant interest the attractive shape beneath the snugly-fitting jeans and pink cotton top. 'I'm Rodney Mason.' He smiled nastily, 'and you must be the dumb female my cousin wants to marry. Can't think why?'

Carly held on to her temper. What an insufferable individual, and to think she'd be working for him! If this job wasn't so important to her she'd leave here and now.

She repeated her earlier question. 'Since when have the milking hours been changed?'

'Since today, that's when, and on my say-so. I'm the one who calls the shots around here so don't you forget it.' His pale eyes fastened on her mutinous face and pretty pink mouth which was now tight with anger.

'You're obviously one of those stupid blondes, so I'll repeat myself. I'm your boss and you do as I say, right? Then we'll get along just fine. I can't be bothered with sassy females. See that you are here on time tomorrow.'

It took every ounce of control not to spit. If he were to be her new boss then for the sake of a good working relationship she would have to make an effort to get on with him.

She said sweetly, 'Message received and understood.'

Rodney Mason then said, 'On second thoughts you can call me Rod, you being female, and all. It's friendlier.'

Carly's stare became glacial. She had no intention of becoming *friendlier* with this jerk. She had no wish to work with him at all, but she wasn't backing out before she'd given the job a chance.

'No thanks. I prefer to stick to the formalities, Mr Mason.'

He gave a wolfish grin. 'We'll see about that, sweetheart. And as for the conditions here, what were you expecting, state-of-the-art? The old man's on his way out.'

Carly swallowed. As a matter of fact,

she hadn't given it much thought. She'd just assumed there would be adequate equipment. 'I take it that the workers milk by hand?'

She glanced around. There didn't appear to be any washing facilities for them, either. So much for hygiene!

'You got it in one.'

Rod Mason wiped sweaty palms on his already filthy jeans. 'If you're that keen you can begin by cleaning out these stalls in time for the next milking at four.'

'I was told five.'

'Four,' he argued.

Carly shrugged. 'Fine by me.'

If she had to be here an hour earlier, that would mean she could leave an hour earlier in the afternoons. It was quite obvious to her that this awful man had deliberately changed the times in order to wrong-foot her on her first day.

'When last were these stalls cleaned?' she asked, hiding her dismay. The concrete floor was a sight to behold and the gutters were clogged with muck.

58

There didn't even appear to be a steam-jet to clean them with.

He shrugged. 'Who knows? It's not my department.'

'Just what is your department then, Mr Mason? Do you run the beef herd?'

He laughed as though she'd told the joke of the century. 'What's left of it, luvvie. That stupid old man can't see what's in front of his very nose.' He gave a conspiratorial wink. 'Between you and me, everything's going down-hill fast.'

'In that case,' Carly told him sweetly, 'both you and I will both be looking for other jobs.'

The pale eyes widened. 'What . . . ?'

'You and I,' Carly repeated, 'will have to move on. It stands to reason, doesn't it? No farm, no job.'

Rod Mason shook his head. A strand of fair hair escaped from his greasy pony tail. 'I'm not going anywhere, lady. When the old man's gone, I'll buy the place. I'm just biding my time. It suits me here, see?'

He rubbed his unshaven chin. 'Like I said, I'm not moving, not for anything. Got a good few things going here, see? I breed a few cattle, sell a few cattle, keep the old man happy. The old fool thinks I'm the bee's knees. No worries.'

Carly thought she saw, all right. The creep was letting things run down deliberately so that he could buy Kosi Park for next to nothing when the time came. As it was, he probably pocketed most of Jasper Campbell's slim profits, or at the very least, sabotaged them.

'Who keeps the books?'

Rod Mason looked startled. 'What books?'

'The farm records, for tax purposes, and so on.'

His pale eyes narrowed in anger. 'We don't need any books here. The old man can't be bothered, see? He's kind of lost interest, you may say . . . no heart left for farming, so he lets me handle everything. No worries.'

'I can see that,' Carly murmured dryly.

Rod preened. 'Just you remember that I'm really the one who calls the shots here, OK? Get moving, then, Miss Smith. You'll have to tackle the stalls by yourself; I can't spare any of the workers to help you.'

'No, I didn't think you could,' Carly concurred sweetly. 'But no worries, as you say, Mr Mason, I'm not afraid of hard work. I'm Cedara trained.'

He started. 'Cedara? You've been to Cedara College?'

'That's what my certificate says.'

Anger flared openly. Or was it fear?

'See to it you don't upset the workforce, then,' he snapped. 'We can do without your stinking high-flown ideas, OK? We do things our way at Kosi Park so watch your step, lady. We don't need the likes of you getting up our noses.'

Silently Carly counted to ten, her fists tightly balled. 'Oh, you need have no fear of that, Mr Mason. You stick to your job and I'll stick to mine, and we'll run along just fine. Excuse me.'

She turned and marched back to the car where she'd left her working gloves and her new green rubber boots. Her hands shook with the force of her feelings as she hauled them on. It was unforgivable!

That nice old man, Jasper Campbell, was being fleeced right under his very nose by that awful man, and the sad thing was that he either didn't know or didn't care.

Rod Mason watched her departure through narrowed eyes. He prided himself on his prowess where women were concerned. Unfortunately women were not exactly thick on the ground in this neck of the woods, but here was an opportunity too good to be missed. Before long he'd have ousted his cousin and taken the woman for himself.

5

Carly arrived back at Jozini Acres just as the sun was dipping behind the hills and the ibises were cawing noisily to their roost at the dam. It was her favourite time of the day, but today she couldn't enjoy the scene to the full. She was dog-tired.

The milking shed at Kosi Park might be spotless, but her arms and shoulders would never be the same again! They ached something awful, and on top of that her nose itched and her eyes were red and puffy from all the dust and muck she'd churned up. However, despite these discomforts Carly was happy. Very happy.

'Hi, Trifina, I'm back,' she sang as she dumped her filthy boots in the utility room next to the kitchen.

Trifina, busy with the evening meal, took one look at her appearance and clucked, 'You had better not let the pilot see you looking like that,' she advised strongly, 'he will not consider you to be a very suitable bride.'

Carly's eyebrows rose. 'What are you talking about?'

Trifina mashed the potatoes, determination in every thump. 'I'm referring to the pilot. That grandson of old Mr Campbell, who is lying in the guest bedroom,' she repeated.

She clicked her tongue, Zulu fashion. 'I remember him as a child. He must be over thirty now, and I can see that he is still not married. That is not good. He must have a bride to comfort him, and you would do very well.'

Carly had forgotten all about their handsome, enigmatic patient. Her heartbeat quickened, and all at once she didn't feel so weary. 'Nonsense, Trifina! I'm not in the market for marriage. Anyway, if he's that old and still not married it's probably because he hates women.'

Trifina stopped her mashing and placed her hands on her hips. 'No, he does not hate women. If he hated women he would not be asking questions about you every time I go near.'

Carly gaped. 'He's been asking about me? What sort of questions? What did you say?'

Trifina's eyes gleamed. She had no intention of revealing just how many praises she'd sung. 'I told him you were a wicked, wicked girl.'

'Thanks for nothing.'

'Dinner,' Trifina warned, turning to place the dish of mashed potatoes in the warmer, 'is almost ready.'

Carly hurried down the passage towards her room. Halfway there she weakened, and tapped softly on the guestroom door. At the grunted reply she opened it and peeped inside.

Jason Edwards appeared to be fast asleep, with Amber cosily ensconced on the covers beside him.

'Amber!' Carly hissed. 'Down! Get off at once.'

Jason opened his eyes. 'Heartless

woman,' he muttered.

He patted Amber's departing rump and slowly hefted himself upright. His gaze rested on Carly's cross face, and then widened as he registered her dirty, unkempt state.

'Good grief. What have we here?'

Carly bridled. 'I work hard for my living,' she said coldly. 'And may I point out that a dog is a dog is a dog! Beds are not made for dogs. Baskets are.'

Jason's mouth twitched. 'I agree with you there.'

'Then kindly do not encourage Amber to disobey an order. I'm having enough trouble training her as it is.'

'Then shall we begin?' Jason suggested. He touched his forelock respectfully. 'Good evening, Miss Smith.'

'And you needn't toady to me, either.'

At her glacial stare he gave a great rumble of laughter, allowing his gaze to rest on the pieces of hay stubble caught in her hair before dropping to the muddy, malodorous socks on her feet.

'It's been some day, by the look of things.' He grinned, wrinkling his nose. 'Ever heard of a shower?'

Carly blushed in mortification. 'You'd smell too if you'd been mucking out a disgracefully neglected cowshed all day,' she retorted. 'Your grandfather has been extremely neglectful. It was a pig of a job!'

Jason jerked upright. 'My grandfather?'

'I believe so, yes. A Mr Jasper Campbell, of Kosi Park,' Carly told him clearly.

Jason's jaw dropped. He passed a hand over his suddenly throbbing eyes and muttered helplessly, 'Either I'm still concussed or you're telling me you've just cleaned out my grandfather's milking parlour, and that it was in a filthy state.'

'That is what I said.'

He frowned. 'My grandfather, I'll have you know, is not in the habit of neglecting anything, least of all his farming operations. However, should you be speaking the truth, may I enquire why you should have done him this enormous favour?'

'I work for him.'

His grey gaze narrowed on her face. 'You mean, as in 'employed', with a pay packet at the end of the week? In heaven's name, why? Why would a girl like you wish to muck out barns? Surely there are other labourers available to do that?' He added wearily, 'Jasper must be crazier than I thought.'

Carly took a deep breath. Not another one! If anything riled her more it was a condescending male who did not understand her driving need to succeed in her chosen career.

'Why is it that you males are so slow?' she exploded. 'Come into the twenty-first century, luvvie!'

Jason regarded her with interest. 'Oops. I've obviously pressed a button.'

'You certainly have,' Carly spat. After all the male opposition in the last twenty-four hours, not to mention the stresses of the day, she'd had altogether enough. 'You men are all the same . . . nothing but a bunch of ego-ridden, condescending, sexist pigs!'

Her chest heaved with the force of her feelings. 'I have news for you, buster. For your information I am both 'book learned' and 'hog smart', as they say!' She spelled it our further, ' . . . as in, 'educated, trained and intelligent.' Get it? If you don't believe a female can do a job just as well as a male then do allow me to enlighten you, my poor man . . . ' She paused for breath.

'My chosen career is agriculture, and I'm both personally and professionally able to run a farm as well as the next man, and that includes your grandfather's dairy herd. I repeat, I am fully qualified in agricultural matters and I have the relevant piece of paper to show for it. Satisfied?'

He digested the information she'd just chucked at him in amazed delight. A more suitable bride he couldn't have found if he'd tried!

'Then accept my apologies, Miss

Smith. You are obviously more than qualified to be a successful farmer. It would appear that you are supremely suited to the position you so patently cherish, and I wish you well in your chosen career.'

The speech was a little flowery, but some pouring of oil on trouble waters was indicated . . . regretfully, because Miss Carly Smith was utterly captivating when she was spitting brimstone.

Jason looked suitably meek and humble, so that Carly's anger disappeared in a puff of smoke. The man was big enough to apologise, which soothed her ego considerably. All she ever wanted was recognition of her abilities and the freedom to get on with her work.

'That's OK.' She sighed. 'I guess I just dumped all my frustrations on you. I'm sorry.'

She gave a sudden smile. It was a smile of great charm, and Jason was floored. His breath caught in his chest and he couldn't have spoken if he'd wanted to.

He shook his head. What was happening to him? The tough, hard-bitten reporter of a week ago was turning into mush. Soft, gooey mush. It was unbelievable!

'Will you excuse me?' Carly begged. 'I shall go and take that shower now because dinner is almost ready and Grandpa likes us to be punctual.'

At the door she turned. 'You may call me Carly,' she said kindly before disappearing.

6

Good morning,' Carly greeted Rod Mason on Wednesday morning as she arrived for work. It was a beautiful morning and she had just enjoyed the sight of the early morning sun gilding the fertile pastures with their thick, wild grasses.

Her boss looked up from lighting a cigarette and didn't bother to reply. 'If you want to keep your job,' he told her sourly, 'you will have to learn to speak Zulu. The men are becoming confused. They can't understand your instructions.'

'I . . . ' Carly began, and closed her mouth with a snap.

Having grown up in the area she was an accomplished Zulu linguist, but she was darned if she'd reveal that fact to Rod Mason. She had her own reason for *playing dumb*. If she wanted to find out what was going on at Kosi Park it would be best to keep her mouth shut and listen to the conversations going on around her, and for this reason she'd been addressing the workers in English, with suitable actions to indicate what she wanted. As far as she was concerned, they understood her perfectly.

'I'm off to the office,' Rod flung over his shoulder as he slunk from the dairy.

Determined not to let the man rile her, Carly set to work. Her strategy was soon rewarded. She was forking fresh hay into the stalls for the cows to munch while they stood patiently giving their milk when she noticed that the Zulu herdsmen were darting furtive glances in her direction. As they worked they spoke in quiet, intense snatches.

On the pretext of inspecting the newly-cleaned byres, Carly inched closer and shamelessly eavesdropped. She was shocked at what she heard.

' . . . more guns . . . '

' . . . enough to start the fight . . . '

'... Boss Mason will get them soon ...'

'... Chief Vuma will find the money to pay ...'

Despite the heat being generated in the shed by the warm breath and bodies of the animals, Carly went cold. Tribal loyalties in this part of the world ran deep, and feuding between the tribal chiefs was a sad fact of life.

She looked up, and immediately the men stopped speaking and became absorbed in their milking. Surely these likeable men and the other workers at Kosi Park were not planning a faction fight with the neighbouring tribe? What if the workers at Jozini Acres were also involved? If so, a great number of people would be harmed. It didn't bear thinking about.

With trembling fingers Carly pretended to scribble some figures on her clipboard while she marshalled her whirling thoughts. It was obvious that Rodney Mason was involved in all this, too.

The only way she could keep Mr Mason under surveillance would be to seek him out more often — if she could bear it — on the pretext of asking his advice about farming matters. But if she found that too galling she could always pretend to be attracted to him, even more hateful as that would be.

Quelling her distaste at the very thought, she nodded to the men and marched from the shed. There was no time to be lost. Her grandfather always said there was no time like the present, and in that case she would begin at once.

★ ★ ★

'I'm deeply grateful to you both for your care and hospitality,' Jason said.

To her surprise, he leaned down and kissed Mary MacDonald on the cheek before extending a large hand towards her husband. Not bothering to hide his reluctance, Daniel MacDonald shook it.

Jason smiled down at his crisp jeans and fresh shirt. 'I have already thanked Trifina for the wonderful meals and my newly-laundered clothing,' he told his hosts, 'she's a gem.'

'A nosey little gem.' Mary laughed. 'She likes to know what is going on. We have to be careful to preserve our privacy at times.'

Jason grinned. He must have given Trifina quite a thrill in the last few days with all his questions about Carly. She'd been endearingly keen to boast about her young mistress's virtues, hinting broadly that Carly would make a good wife.

'Well, I'll be off. Thank you once again. After all your cosseting,' he told Mary, 'I feel like a new man.'

She waved away his thanks. 'Think nothing of it, dear. It was the least we could do for our nearest neighbour. We isolated farmers must stick together and help one another out.' Ignoring her husband's frown, she added, 'You are welcome to come back and visit us at any time, Jason.'

Jason nodded his thanks. If only she knew! He intended to become a frequent visitor in the weeks ahead.

His two suitcases had been destroyed in the blaze so he would need to visit the town of Jozini as soon as possible in order to kit himself out. What a pleasure it would be, he reflected, to exchange his jackets and ties for some khaki bush clothes. Until then he would simply have to make use of the old clothing he'd left at Kosi Park.

He climbed into the truck and was driven away by Joseph, Daniel's driver, in an old pick-up truck. The Zulu appeared to be deep in troubled thought and preserved a stolid silence all the way to Kosi Park where he deposited Jason at the farm gates before disappearing again in a cloud of dust.

At that moment Jason's cell phone sounded. 'Where the heck is that report?' James O'Brien demanded. 'I haven't heard a word from you. May I remind you that I have a newspaper to sell? I suppose now that you've tendered your resignation you think you can sit on your whatsit.'

'Good morning, sir,' Jason responded politely, curbing his irritation. 'I'll be investigating the matter as soon as I possibly can. I've only just arrived at Kosi Park this minute.' Briefly he explained the situation.

'Well, don't sit around,' the editor growled.

Jason hadn't expected to hear, 'I'm sorry to hear you nearly lost your life,' or any similar token of concern, and it only confirmed to him that his decision to leave the journalistic rat-race had been the correct one.

He pocketed his phone and looked about him with interest at the vast pastures where one or two cows grazed at will. It was puzzling to see so few animals around. On his last visit five years ago the fields had been full of fat, healthy cattle with gleaming coats and full udders.

The gateposts needed a coat of paint

and there was a strand of wire missing from the fence but these were minor things; they would be attended to once he had settled in. He trudged up the long drive to his grandfather's homestead with the old, familiar smell of the veldt strong in his nostrils.

Red dust settled in the back of his throat but it was a welcome taste; far better than the murky, polluted atmosphere of the cities he'd worked in. Sudden happiness warmed his heart in the way that the sunshine was warming his back. He was glad to be back!

The farmhouse hove into view around the next bend, and Jason's smile disappeared. He stood in stunned incomprehension, and just stared.

'What the blazes . . . ?'

The old man had obviously slipped a cog!

' . . . Gone nutty as a bag of circus peanuts,' he muttered. How can he have let things go like this? Where in the name of all Africa had that Campbell pride disappeared to?

Savagely he kicked the dirt at his feet. In the short years since he'd last visited Kosi Park it had turned into a dilapidated mess. He hadn't realised his grandfather had been that keen on heading for the retirement pasture!

Jason hastened up the veranda steps to the front door, not quite sure whether to bang the heavy brass knocker or walk right in. He settled for banging the knocker.

Joyce Thembisa, the Zulu housekeeper, stared at him in surprise.

'Good morning. Is my grandfather in?'

Recognition dawned. A beam split her black face. 'Ah. You are the grandson. You have come home at last. He has been waiting a very long time.'

Disconcerted, Jason followed her down the passage to the living-room he remembered so well. Had his grandfather really been longing for his return? Well, he'd come back for good now, and he intended to make it up to the old man.

Jasper Campbell was reading a newspaper with the aid of a magnifying glass. As he looked up his eyes widened behind the thick lenses of his spectacles.

'Jason?'

With some difficulty he rose to his feet and extended a hand, then as though his grandson had only been away a few weeks he said, 'I was just reading your last article on Iraq. I always keep up with your travels, you know. Get the Natal News delivered at the end of each week in a batch from the newsagent in Jozini.'

A lump lodged itself suddenly in Jason's throat. The old man was looking frailer than he'd expected. Small wonder he'd allowed the farm to go to rack and ruin.

He gripped the old man's hand fiercely and smiled in order to hide his emotion. 'How are you?'

'Me? I've never been better. Sit down, sit down, lad. How long can you stay?'

'That depends on you, but I'd rather hoped I could come home for good.'

Jasper's eyes widened. 'For good?'

'Yes. It's about time, isn't it? I'm here to help you all I can, Grandfather. I've resigned from the newspaper. I intend to learn how to run the farm so that we can restore Kosi Park to its former glory, and I'm prepared to work hard. Will you have me?'

The tired blue eyes blazed with sudden vigour. 'Get away with you, lad.' He laughed. 'Kosi Park is your inheritance. I can now hand it over to you, and it will be an enormous relief. See that you do a good job.'

'Oh, I intend to.'

'You'll need to find a wife, Jason,' his grandfather advised a moment later. 'Farming's difficult enough as it is. A good woman at your side can lighten the load.'

Jason agreed gravely. 'I intend to do that, too, Grandfather.'

'Then we shall celebrate your home-coming with a wee dram, shall we not?'

The old man reached for his stick, hobbled over to the drinks cabinet and chose a bottle of the finest.

'At ten in the morning?' Jason teased.

'Aye. I've been waiting for this day ever since you went away to the university.' He sloshed a generous amount of whisky into two tumblers, added a little water and handed one to his grandson. 'Welcome home, laddie.'

Jason, who hated whisky, drained his glass like a good Scotsman.

'Thank you,' he muttered, trying not to cough.

Jasper watched him and laughed. 'No need to slug your drink in that fashion, laddie. You'll have to slow down; you're still going at the city's pace. You're in the country now, where we live by the rhythms of nature.'

'I daresay I'll get used to it, Grandfather, but I'm not one to allow the grass to grow under my feet. When I make up my mind about something, I go for it.'

'Aye, you've always known exactly

what you wanted.'

'May I have my old bedroom?'

'Certainly. Ask Joyce to make up a fresh bed, and then take a look around, if you like.'

Jason clapped his grandfather on the back. 'That is exactly what I intend to do. The sooner I can get things moving here, the better. I'd particularly like to examine your . . . I mean our . . . dairy operation.'

Jasper leaned back in his chair and waved a hand. 'Feel free, Jason. You won't find it up to much, I'm afraid, but we'll start rebuilding our stock again as from next week. As for the beef herd . . . ' his eyes held renewed hope and purpose, 'we can only go from strength to strength now that you're back.'

Jason felt humbled by his grandfather's confidence in him. 'I sincerely hope so, Grandfather.'

'I daresay we can let the farm manager go in due course . . . an unsavoury character by the name of

Rodney Mason. He's no great shakes at the job so it'll be no loss . . . thinks I can't see how lazy he is.' He grew thoughtful. 'I've just employed a grand little lass in the dairy . . . I suppose we can dismiss her, too, when her month's trial is up.'

The unaccustomed whisky was burning a hole in Jason's gut. He gave a small hiccup. 'I wouldn't do anything too hastily, Grandfather,' he advised, concealing a grin. 'If she's any good she may well be an asset to both of us.'

'True.'

Feeling a little light-headed, Jason floated to the door.

'I'll go this very minute and check her out.'

7

Some men, Carly reflected smugly as she went in search of Rodney Mason, were dumber than a wagonload of rocks, especially the likes of her boss. He was that dumb, he'd sell his horse to buy horse feed.

All she had to do now was to play up to him, make him notice her as a woman. She'd bet the farm and all its cattle that he'd fall for it like hay off a swerving lorry.

As she left the dairy she allowed herself a small, secret chuckle. By conveying her interest in him she would allay any suspicions he might have of her prying into his life, which was exactly what she intended to do. Before long she would know precisely what he was up to, and when she had her facts straight she'd hightail it to the police station at Jozini.

She knocked on the office door and went in. Her boss was nowhere to be seen. Carly looked about her in disgust. The room was a shambles, with books, files and farming magazines lying scattered about on every available surface. The drawers of a metal filing cabinet were standing open and dirty coffee mugs lined the dusty windowsill. It was exactly what one would have expected from the likes of Mr Mason!

'Yuk,' she muttered, and closed the door.

Eventually Carly located her boss behind the tractor shed. He was leaning against the wall, smoking.

By now it was mid-morning. He should, Carly thought angrily, be out in the fields supervising the weaning of the calves. The little animals had just been separated from their mothers and were bawling their heads off in a nearby pasture. It made her very angry to see them being neglected so heartlessly.

It would appear that Rod Mason was not only dumb; he was bone idle, too.

Old *never-sweats* was in the habit of avoiding all responsibility, that much was obvious. Why in heaven's name did Jasper Campbell continue to employ him?

Carly was determined that when she'd finished acting the charming bimbo she'd march out and supervise the calves' feeding herself. Rod Mason could think what he liked!

'Oh, hello, Mr Mason,' she cooed. 'Having a moment's respite from your busy schedule? Can't say I blame you.'

His pale eyes narrowed on her shapely form. 'What do you want?'

Carly giggled. 'A moment's respite from my busy schedule.' She rolled her eyes heavenwards and confided, 'that awful old man has been bothering me again.'

Rod Mason's head snapped up. 'Jasper? Fancies you, does he?' He guffawed like a double-jawed hyena. 'There must be life in the dirty old dog, after all!'

Carly flushed angrily. Trust a mind

like Mason's to follow that disgusting track! Jasper Campbell was no lecherous old man, he was a charming old dear!

'Oh, no,' she corrected him, 'it's nothing like that; it's to do with work. He keeps saying I'm to ask your advice when I don't know something, so I've come to ask.' It was a barefaced lie and Carly felt uncomfortable uttering it. She knew her job inside out and on the past three days showing it was obvious that Rodney Mason was the incompetent one.

Rod stubbed out his cigarette rather carelessly on the wall of the shed and immediately lit another. He inhaled a lungful of smoke and rasped, 'What is it you want to know?'

Carly thought quickly. 'Oh, nothing, really. That was just an excuse.'

'Come again?'

'An excuse,' she repeated shamelessly, 'to see you. May I call you Rod? I don't have any questions about work, really.'

He stared. 'Why would you want to see me?'

Carly giggled once more. 'Why not? You're a very attractive man.'

A knowing smile spread itself over his coarse features. The woman was falling for him already! Wait till he told his stupid cousin, Grant. The guy would be that jealous he'd start snapping like a turtle.

'Bored, huh?' He moved like lightning and slipped a sweaty arm around Carly's shoulders.

Hastily Carly twisted from his embrace, contriving to look sweetly flustered. 'Not during working hours, Rod,' she implored. 'Some other time, perhaps?'

'Then how about you and me spending a little time together after work? I'll meet you down by the river.'

She dimpled coquettishly. 'I don't like rivers.' Not when they were as isolated as this one was, at any rate. She had no intention of deliberately placing herself in any danger.

'I'd rather come to your cottage,

Rod. We can sit on the veranda and have a drink. Shall we say just after five?'

'Five it is, then.' He drew deeply on his cigarette. 'Now scram and get on with your work.'

Only too happy to escape, Carly turned around and immediately cannoned into another masculine body; one, she realised in considerable relief, which smelled of soap and water.

'Oh! It's you,' she gasped.

Blandly Jason viewed her from his great height. 'Yes, it's me. I am sorry to interrupt your little rendezvous.'

He looked from Rod Mason to Carly, who looked away in embarrassment. Her dewy cheeks sported a very becoming blush, so that Jason had difficulty in removing his gaze. She looked even lovelier today, he reflected with masculine satisfaction. He rather hoped her lack of composure was the result of seeing him, but it could have been due to that lout who'd been about to kiss her.

'What . . . what are you doing here?' Carly managed.

'I live here.'

'You mean . . . here? At Kosi Park?' He was supposed to live in Durban, according to Trifina. The housekeeper had taken to quizzing him shamelessly and then informing Carly of her findings.

'Where else?'

'But . . . why are you not in bed at Jozini Acres?'

'Because I'm now fully recovered and fighting fit. Ready, in fact, for some good, hard work.'

Jason turned to the man slouching against the wall. 'You must be Mason.'

Rod shuffled to his feet and glared back aggressively. 'Who are you?'

'I'm your new boss, Mason, and I don't like my employees standing about wasting time, holding up shed walls. I suggest you get on with whatever it is you're supposed to be doing' he clipped.

Rod gaped stupidly. 'Boss . . . ? But

I'm the boss here.'

'No longer. My name is Jason Edwards, and as from today Kosi Park belongs to me.'

'On whose say-so?'

'My grandfather's.'

Light dawned. Rod Mason spat on the grass in disgust. 'You're Jasper Campbell's grandson!'

'Yes.'

'The old snake!' Rod said bitterly, 'he never said anything . . . '

'Get weaving, Mason,' Jason ordered shortly. 'I'll expect a full report from you on all farming activities by the end of next week; that gives you a whole ten days to get your act together. On Monday I shall expect to view all records. Is that clear?'

'There are no records.' The pale eyes flashed shiftily. 'The old man couldn't be bothered . . . I've never seen any . . . I mean . . . ' Rod stammered.

'Then we will have to bring in a firm of accountants to rectify matters,' Jason told him silkily.

Rod tried to hide his alarm, relying on bravado. 'Do what you like, I couldn't care less!' He flung his cigarette stub down and strode away. As soon as he'd wrapped up his latest little deal, he'd be out of here . . .

'That man's like a catfish,' Jason murmured to himself as he watched the bristling retreat, 'all mouth and no brains.'

Carly rounded on him. 'Just who do you think you are? You can't come in here and start high-handedly ordering everyone about.'

Jason's mouth twitched. He watched her march back to the cowshed and because he wanted to observe her activities more closely, followed at a leisurely pace. Carly Smith, he reflected with a grin, was turning out to be the spice of his life.

Furious with herself at having been caught in what must seem to Jason Campbell a compromising situation with her boss, Carly attacked the already spotless stalls with a broom while her thoughts tumbled about furiously in her head. It was a good ten minutes before she calmed down.

'Feeling better?' Jason asked.

Carly's head snapped up. He was leaning against the door of the shed, obviously enjoying himself.

'Now who's idling his life away, holding up the shed?' she demanded hotly. 'Haven't you anything better to do? Just how long have you been standing there?'

Jason's eyes gleamed. 'Long enough to be able to give an excellent report of your work to my grandfather.'

'I am not in the habit of working for a boss who spies on his employees,' Carly said coldly. She placed her hands on her hips and looked him up and down. 'If, in fact, you really are the new owner.'

If he was, things were moving altogether too fast for her. 'I can assure you that I am.'

He sauntered across to the wall where Carly had hung her file, unclipped it and asked with interest, 'is this a record of the week's milk yield?'

'It is.'

He studied it carefully before handing it back. Naturally it made no sense at all to his untrained eye. 'Carly,' he said quietly, 'I can see that this dairy is not in a good state. I'm hoping to build it up again and I'd appreciate any suggestions you might have.'

Carly nodded. 'Well, as a matter of fact, I have several. With regard to good milk cows . . . ' she reeled off a number of facts and figures about where to obtain suitable cattle, which kind and at what price.

'Hmmm. Impressive,' Jason murmured. She had obviously done her homework.

'Apart from buying new cows, how do we go about upgrading our existing strains?'

'Easy. We give our cows the best possible chance of conceiving by feeding them well. So you see,' she finished, 'stockmanship is very crucial in all of this.'

Jason was looking awfully blank. Carly's large brown eyes narrowed in sudden suspicion.

'Which agricultural college did you train at?'

He shrugged. 'I didn't.'

'I beg your pardon . . . ?'

'I have a degree in English and Political Science. I know nothing whatsoever about farming, Carly Smith, so I'll be relying heavily on you to put me straight.'

Carly's mouth dropped open. Sweet heaven, was she to work alongside yet another ignoramus? That made two morons, one useless old man and a pile of dilapidated stones they called buildings. Was she insane to work here, or what?

She took a deep, calming breath. If it wasn't for her MacDonald pride and the fact that she desperately wanted to find out about this impending faction fight, she'd walk out here and now.

'I don't think . . . ' she began firmly, and trailed off in confusion. Jason was smiling down at her in a heart-stopping manner and it was causing an alarming buzzing noise in her head. Her blood seemed to have turned into a bubbling warmth.

Jason leaned forward and placed a fingertip against her lips in order to stop what looked to be the beginnings of another diatribe.

'Shall we agree to a truce? I know you're a MacDonald and I'm a Campbell, but surely we can work together? The two clans were at one time sworn enemies, but we have no wish to repeat things. I daresay you know your Scottish history?'

'No. I was born in Africa and my parents never spoke of such things. Why should they? It was a long time ago. Anyway, there is enough tribal in-fighting in these parts amongst the Zulu people to occupy our attention.'

'Unfortunately that is true. But we're discussing us, Carly. What about that truce?'

Carly started to shove him away. 'I

— I'm not sure . . . '

Jason lifted her chin with his fingertips and looked steadily into her eyes. 'I need you, Carly,' he told her clearly. If only she knew how much! 'Will you help me run this farm?'

The full force of his magnetism completely enveloped her so that she was unable to look away. Beside the effect of his disturbing proximity, the offer was extremely tempting. If she agreed to his request then together they could turn Kosi Park into a model of state-of-the-art efficiency; a challenge which was almost impossible to resist.

Ideas like snowflakes were beginning to feather about in her head, she had so many of them that her mind was spinning. If she agreed to help him, it would mean she'd have a free hand to implement all the latest trends. Carly Smith, Farmer, would be in heaven!

'I will,' she promised breathlessly, her bright gaze filled with eager anticipation.

Jason hid his relief. 'Thank you.'

99

The sight of Carly's moist lips, slightly parted, was irresistible. He found it difficult to tell which of them moved first, but the next moment Carly was in his arms, locked in an embrace he wished could last forever.

Without reservation Carly gave herself up to his kiss. When he felt her response, Jason deepened it . . . insisting without demanding.

Instinctively Carly snuggled closer. She'd been kissed before, but never like this.

'Jason . . . ' she murmured, and then pulled away. It would not do to forget who and where she was. She was an employee, and this man was her new boss. To find herself in his arms while on the job was hardly a professional way to act.

She stared up at him, trying to hide her swirling emotions. She'd never felt this way about a man before, never even considered that it was possible to be so affected by another individual. It was a new and wholly delicious sensation, and if this was love, she had it badly. She shook her head, blinked a few times and tried to pull herself together.

Jason, watching her, cleared his throat. 'Uh . . . yes, maybe we'd better stop right there.'

As his breathing steadied he concluded, 'I'd say our pact was sealed, wouldn't you?'

It had given him immense satisfaction to discover that underneath all that sassy independence Carly wasn't nearly as prim as she appeared to be. She wasn't quite as immune to him as she wanted him to think, either.

Remembering his determination to make her fall in love with him, he decided there was no time like the present to start the wining and dining.

'May I take you out to dinner this evening, Carly? I believe there's a new restaurant in Jozini and we might like to try it.'

Carly's face fell. 'I'm sorry, but I will be visiting Rod Mason after work today.' A boring visit it would be, too.

How could she bear to spend even one moment in Rod's company after having been in Jason's arms? But she had a purpose to fulfil, and fulfil it she would. She wouldn't be a farmer today if she were the type of person who backed down from an unpleasant task.

Jason was not the jealous type, but he found it difficult to control the sudden anger which sent his blood pressure into overdrive. Could she not see what a louse Rod Mason was?

'Some other time, then,' he agreed blandly.

'Yes. Some other time.'

Carly watched him stride from the shed, her heart and mind in turmoil. The unsettling jumble of thoughts and emotions had left her feeling positively weak. How could she put her mind to her job after this?

8

Well?' Jasper enquired when his grandson had seated himself at the dining-table for lunch. 'Did you see that grand little lass I was telling you about?'

'I saw her, Grandfather.'

'And?'

Jason looked up. He said blandly, 'I intend to marry her.'

Shrewd blue eyes regarded him with a twinkle. 'Aren't you being a little hasty?'

'No.'

'You've only just met her.'

'Wrong, Grandfather. I met her at the beginning of the week.'

'Even so, that's hardly a lifetime. Remember the old adage, 'marry in haste, and repent at leisure?' I shouldn't be in too much of a hurry if I were you. We know nothing of her background; who her parents are and where she comes from.'

'Don't worry; I know what I'm doing.'

'Did you meet her in Durban?'

Jasper forked Joyce's delicious fish pie into his mouth and chewed it thoughtfully. Now for the interesting part . . .

'No,' he said deliberately, 'I met her on Daniel MacDonald's farm, Jozini Acres.'

Jasper went pale. 'What the dickens were you doing there?'

Jason swallowed his mouthful and forked another. 'I was staying there as a houseguest.'

His grandfather choked. He slammed a fist down on the table. 'What were you doing on MacDonald property? Why go fiddling about in the home of my enemy? It beggars belief that you would do such a thing, Jason.'

Jason gave a great, inward sigh. He had hoped that his grandfather had mellowed a little, but that was obviously not the case. The feud was as strong as ever.

'Grandfather, the MacDonalds were very kind to me. I was concussed as a result of an accident and they took me in.'

'Accident? What accident?'

Briefly he explained the situation. 'So you see, I had nowhere to land the plane. What else could I do but put her down on MacDonald property? I had no idea you'd dispensed with that airfield. Quite frankly, I'm glad to be alive.'

Jasper was silent for a few moments.

He cleared his throat and said gruffly, 'We'll not talk of it further, Jason. The matter is closed.'

'Fine by me.'

'You'll need some form of transport now, will you not?'

'I was hoping you'd let me use one of the farm vehicles.'

Jasper shook his white head. 'The Mercedes and the Land-Rover were sold a while ago. I can no longer drive and they were rotting away in the garage, so I instructed Rodney Mason to get rid of them, but I must say he didn't get a very good price. There's only the pick-up truck, which the staff use, in which case we'll have to make another purchase. You can go into Jozini whenever you like, there's a reliable car dealer in the main street.'

Jason searched his grandfather's face. He put down his fork and said carefully, 'Can we afford to?'

'Good heavens, yes. I know it looks otherwise, but my bank balance is very healthy. It's just that I've had no interest in anything . . . '

'I understand.'

He rose and poured his grandfather a cup of coffee from the silver pot which Joyce had left on the sideboard. It was an immense relieve to know the old man wasn't quite the pauper he'd imagined him to be, but where had the money come from? Astute farm management in the past, or some other source, perhaps?

He drank his own coffee with a bland face which concealed the disturbing thoughts behind it. His spirits sank further as he remembered the reason he'd agreed to come to Kosi Park in the first place; to unravel the mystery of the illegal immigrants crossing the border, and the farmer who was ostensibly making money out of them. He could still not quite believe that his grandfather was involved, but he would keep an open mind. That was what proper journalism was all about.

Jason drained his cup and excused himself from the table. He made his way to the two-roomed office building adjacent to the farmhouse, determined to spend the afternoon rooting about for any old farm records, which may or may not be there. After that he intended to make some enquiries about a reliable firm of accountants who would handle the books in future. The sooner things were on a sound legal and financial footing, the better.

His thoughts returned to Carly. As soon as he'd solved this immigrants business he'd be able to concentrate on his love life. His intention was to make Carly Smith his bride by the end of the year, and it was already October.

When he was finished in the office, Jason decided, he would take a walk in the vicinity of Rod Mason's cottage. His darling might think it was perfectly in order to join the man for an innocent aperitif after a long, hot day at work, but she couldn't possibly understand the mind workings of a creep like that. She might well be letting herself in for more than she'd bargained . . .

9

Carly tidied herself as best she could in one of the farmhouse bathrooms and looked about her with interest as she headed for the side door which led out into the garden. It was a charming old place but it lacked a woman's touch. It was a great pity Kosi Park had no mistress.

For a moment, Carly fell prey to some delightful dreams. If she lived here it would naturally be as the wife of Jason Edwards. At the very thought, her heartbeat skittered. They'd have a magnificent wedding, fix up the old house and fill it with four or five children; sturdy little boys who looked like Jason and little girls with long, fair braids who looked like her. They'd buy a couple of ponies for the children and build a swimming pool and a tennis court, and . . .

'Oh dear, you are getting carried away, Carly Smith,' she mocked.

To distract herself from such an improbable scenario she turned her thoughts to the gracious old rooms which were crying out for redecoration. She'd take great pleasure in restoring them to their former glory without delay.

An antique George IV sofa here, a mahogany inlaid desk there, A Victorian chaise longue before the bow window in the living-room; not to mention all that glorious silver on the sideboard and the walnut long case grandfather clock in the hall. She'd seen some old country chairs in an antique shop in Jozini recently, with a lovely rich patina and rush seats. They'd bring such warmth and texture to the dining-room . . .

'Get a grip, Carly!' she muttered.

Kosi Park would never be her home! She was a career girl, here to do a farming job, and that was that. She might be wildly attracted to Jason Edwards but she had to remember just who he was. Her grandfather would have a blue fit if he knew she was in love with a Campbell!

As she headed for Rod Mason's cottage Carly tried not to feel revulsion at the thought of spending an hour in the man's company. It would be important to keep him talking, which shouldn't be too difficult; all she had to do was introduce the subject of Rod Mason, himself.

He was one of those dim, arrogant self-serving men who imagined the little woman existed solely to laugh at his jokes.

'The things I do for Africa . . . ' She sighed..

As it turned out, Rod was standing under a nearby tree, deep in conversation with two of the Zulu labourers. When he heard her footsteps on the concrete path he looked up and frowned.

'Oh, I'd forgotten you were coming,' he told her rudely.

Quite! thought Carly.

Rod waved her carelessly on to the veranda and grunted, 'Be with you in a moment.'

Carly nodded and smiled, and seated herself on one of the cane chairs. Acting the bimbo, she took out a small mirror from her handbag and pretended to be completely fascinated by her own looks, and then re-applied her lipstick.

When seemingly satisfied with the result, she began to powder her nose, all the time straining to hear what the men were saying. Out of the corner of her eye she noticed how the Zulus kept darting furtive glances in her direction.

'Don't worry,' she heard Rod tell the men confidently, 'she doesn't know a word of Zulu. Carry on . . . '

'Are you sure she cannot understand?'

'Yes,' he snapped. 'You were saying . . . ?'

'Chief Vuma wants to know when you can let him have those guns.'

'In a hurry, is he?'

'We want to attack Chief Langa's

112

kraal on Sunday.'

'Well, you can tell the chief from me that he'll get the guns when he's able to pay for them. I don't allow credit, see.'

'The chief thinks you are lying,' one of the men stated. 'He thinks you do not have the guns.'

Rod swore roundly. 'The chief's a fool! I have the firearms, all right, and I'll have more by tomorrow. I'm expecting three more men from Mozambique tonight and they should have three guns each. That makes it up to at least two dozen I can let the chief have, but I repeat, money first!'

'We will tell him.'

'You can tell him to move it, too. I'm in a hurry. If he leaves it till next week I may not be able to help him.'

'Why is that?'

Rod swore again. 'Never you mind. Let's just say I may have changed my mind.' What he actually meant was that there was a possibility he'd not be around. With that grandson of Jasper's nosing around day after day demanding records and suchlike, it could well be the end of the road for Rodney T. Mason . . .

The men conferred for a moment between themselves.

'We will bring the money tomorrow night at eight o'clock, and you will give us the guns then.'

'See that you do.' Rod growled. 'Now scram!'

Hastily Carly picked up a magazine which had been lying on the table and pretended to read it.

'What'll you have?' Rod enquired as he joined her on the veranda, 'wine or beer?'

'Do you have a soft drink?' In the light of what she'd just heard, Carly decided she'd need all her wits around her.

'No, I haven't. You'll have to have beer,' he told her shortly.

He disappeared into the cottage and returned with two bottles and a glass. With barely concealed anger he poured Carly's drink into the glass and then took a swig from the other bottle. His conversation with the two men appeared to have left him in a bad mood.

Carly smiled sympathetically. 'Having trouble with the labourers?'

'Just a problem about the cattle feed,' he clipped before taking a long slurp. He wiped his mouth on the back of his hand and looked at her with interest. A slow smile spread over his face.

'Like me, do you?'

Carly almost choked. Quickly she changed the subject. 'I've been reading an interesting article in this magazine here, it's all about people having holidays in exotic places.' She sighed loudly. 'I'd love to go on holiday right this moment. I could do with a break from work, couldn't you?'

'Sure. Perhaps we can take one together. Where to?'

'Well, it says here that there are some good beaches in Mozambique.'

Rod's head jerked up. 'Mozambique?' He gave a condescending laugh. 'I wouldn't waste my time.'

115

'Why, don't you like Mozambique?' Carly enquired innocently. 'I've never been there so I can't say.'

'I've been there once or twice.'

'Oh, do tell me all about it,' she begged. 'I think you're so brave, Rod, driving all those miles on roads like that, but I suppose there's nothing much you're afraid of, is there?'

His chest swelled. Females like this one were so easily impressed!

'Nothing much, no. I'd say I'm the adventurous type. I've been pretty much everywhere and done everything,' he boasted.

She gazed at him admiringly. 'You have? I believe that Mozambique is very run down now. I mean, after that Marxist regime and the last war . . .'

'Yeah. It's a mess.'

'Really? I suppose a lot of the people have been left very poor.'

Rod grinned. 'They'd do anything for money.'

Carly seized her opportunity. 'Like what?'

'Oh, they kill the animals and sell the skins. They also sell curios, elephant tusks, wood carvings . . . whatever they can get their hands on.'

'What about all those ex-soldiers? There must be any amount of guns and ammunition floating about. They could sell them for food.'

For a moment she thought she'd gone too far. Rod froze. 'What would you know about things like that?' He took another swig from the bottle. 'You're far too nosey a female for my liking.'

She smiled winningly. 'Am I? It's just that I'm awfully interested in where you've been, and so on.'

'Let's forget about Mozambique, sweetheart. It's a dump, take it from me. We'll talk about you, instead.'

Carly's eyes widened in mock dismay. 'Oh, dear, no. I have a meeting with Mr Campbell up at the house in five minutes. What about tomorrow evening? Say, eight o'clock?'

Rod hesitated. Thoughtfully he fingered his one silver earring. 'I'm busy at eight. Come at nine.'

'Fine.'

She looked at her watch and groaned. 'How time does fly when one is enjoying oneself! I'll have to leave now. Thank you for the drink, Rod. I really must fly . . . '

With a cheery wave she grabbed her handbag and tripped from the veranda.

In frustration Rod flung his empty bottle down on the grass. He grabbed Carly's drink which was still almost full and drained the glass in one go. Stupid woman, wasting good beer!

For want of anything better to do, he picked up the magazine she'd discarded and began to leaf through it.

'Phew, what a creep,' Carly breathed as she high-tailed it up the path. It had been worth the trouble, however. She now knew exactly what was going on at Kosi Park and it sickened her. If all went well, by the time it came for their so-called assignation at nine o'clock tomorrow night, Rod Mason would be wearing his latest jewellery; handcuffs!

She hadn't gone very far when she heard heavy breathing behind her. 'Hold it right there,' Rod panted.

Carly spun around. 'Yes?'

One hand shot out and roughly gripped her arm. 'I've been reading that magazine and there's no such article about holidays in Mozambique. You're a little liar, aren't you? What exactly are you up to?'

His face was only inches from hers and it was ugly with menace.

Carly had no option but to brazen it out. 'Yes, there was,' she told him firmly, 'but not in that particular magazine. Did I not make that clear? It was in the magazine I was reading at lunch time, in my car. I'll show it to you, if you like. Anyway, what's the big deal? If you say that Mozambique's a dump, on your say-so I won't go there, will I?'

She gave him an adoring smile. 'I trust your judgement, Rod.'

He released her arm but continued to frown, apparently undecided.

'Well, just see that you do,' he grated. 'I can't be bothered with females who meddle in my business.'

Carly released the breath she'd been holding. 'I'll see you tomorrow night, then, Rod.'

He glared at her. 'Yeah.'

It was time to lay on the charm. 'I may seem to be a bit nosey I'm just a harmless female,' she simpered, 'what do I know about anything?'

Heavens, she'd had just about enough of making like a dizzy bimbo!

Just then Jason shot out of the bushes. 'Hello,' he greeted them blandly. 'Nice evening, isn't it?'

Rod sprang back. 'Huh?' he squinted.

Jason affected surprise. 'Oh, it's you, Mason ... Miss Smith. Sorry to interrupt your little scene, but I didn't expect to find anyone standing in the middle of the pathway like this.'

Carly took a deep breath and wiped her lips surreptitiously with the back of her hand, an action which caused Jason's mouth to twitch. The poor girl was as white as a sheet.

She said with immense dignity, 'Good evening, Mr Edwards,' and fled.

Keeping Carly in sight, Jason nodded to his frustrated farm manager and proceeded up the path at a leisurely pace. It gave him ample opportunity to think.

From the cover of a large shrub near Rod's cottage he had heard all he wanted to know. How unscrupulous could the man get? He was smuggling impoverished immigrants into the country in exchange for the arms they brought with them, then sold them on illegally to whoever he could; in this case one of the Zulu tribal chiefs to be used for no good purpose. On Sunday, unless that faction fight could be averted, innocent people would lose their lives.

Unfortunately he had been too far away to be able to hear the conversation between Carly and Rod on the veranda. And then he'd stepped out of the bushes and found her in Rod's arms!

Granted she'd looked a little shaken,

but perhaps she'd actually been enjoying the creep's advances. After all, he'd clearly heard her say she couldn't wait for them to be together again tomorrow night.

Jason's firm lips tightened.

He reminded himself that he must keep an open mind and weigh the evidence before him like a good journalist should. He was used to analysing situations objectively, and he must not be swayed by emotions or a pretty face.

Well, he reflected morosely, that evidence was now crystal clear. What it revealed was that he'd been a besotted fool! Carly was not what she seemed. Far from being the sweet, sensible, hard-working girl he'd imagined, she was undoubtedly a callous, unscrupulous little minx who was keen to line her pockets any way she could. Was she expecting Rod to give her a cut out of their latest 'arms deal'?

One good thing he'd discovered was that his grandfather was still the honourable man he'd always believed him to be. The farm records he'd perused for most of the afternoon had been kept meticulously right up until Rod Mason had come to work at Kosi Park two years ago.

10

From then on it was clear that the operation had deteriorated, and combination of mismanagement and fraud had sabotaged the profits. With his health failing and no-one to help him, it was little wonder that his lonely old grandfather had lost heart.

Jason quickened his pace. When he arrived at the homestead he noted that Carly's red Mini was nowhere to be seen.

The question now remained of what he would do with his newly-acquired knowledge. Obviously he would have to go to the police first thing in the morning, and after that he would keep a firm eye on Carly and her boyfriend for the rest of the day until the whole business could be wrapped up.

Feeling thoroughly frustrated, he turned and went into the house, intent on making a start on his report for James O'Brien. He would leave Carly's name out of it because to be fair, at this stage he had no actual proof of her guilt. Besides, he had to admit to a blind, unreasoning urge to protect her.

Jason gave a rueful smile.

It was a good thing his grandfather had no knowledge of what the 'grand little lass' in the dairy was up to, because if he knew he'd probably say something like, 'what else can you expect from a MacDonald? Sack the woman!'

Carly scuttled up the path to the red Mini, her cheeks burning with shame. She could only hope that Jason hadn't witnessed the way she'd so shamelessly led Rod Mason on.

Whatever must he think? That she was some man-starved little female on the make?

Carly slammed the door, revved the engine and roared down the drive, angry with the whole situation. Her only comfort was the thought that the despicable Rod would soon be getting his come-uppance.

If she hadn't been expected home for dinner in half an hour, she'd have driven straight into Jozini to report her findings to the police there and then. As it was, she'd have to beg time off work tomorrow to perform the unpleasant deed.

The Mini swept through the gates of Jozini Acres and as she watched the glorious sunset painting its colours over the western sky, Carly relaxed. The enduring permanence of the distant mountains and the timeless beauty of the vast landscape about her poured their tranquillity into her ruffled emotions.

She told herself sternly that she must keep things in proportion. Rod Mason's imminent arrest wasn't her only comfort after all. She could also take pride in the knowledge that she'd averted an awful tribal conflict and helped promote peace and stability in the area. All in all, it was well worth it.

Jason drove home from Jozini in the brand-new silver Mercedes he had just purchased, feeling more than happy with this morning's work. After a visit to a menswear store to acquire a new set of clothing, he'd spent an interesting hour at the police station with his old friend, Detective Inspector Jeff Morgan.

'You have simply confirmed our suspicions,' his friend told him. 'We have had the situation under surveillance for some time, Mister Mason being our chief suspect. Unfortunately we have not been able to make any arrests without sufficient proof, but after tonight's work we'll be in a position to charge him.'

Jason nodded. 'I'll be waiting for you.'

'See you at six-thirty, then. I'd like to have the men in place well beforehand.'

On his return to Kosi Park Jason parked the car outside the front veranda and went in search of his grandfather.

'Come and take a look at what I've bought, Grandfather,' he enthused, 'she's a beauty. I've also ordered the Land-Rover you requested; dark green. With luck it should be here by next week.'

Jasper reached for his stick and hobbled on to the veranda where the two men stood in admiration for the next ten minutes, debating the merits of the new satellite-linked direction finder and other new-fangled gadgets.

'They come as standard on this model,' Jason was explaining happily. He broke off abruptly as Carly came around the corner. At the sight of her his heart set up a wild hammering which interfered with his breathing in a most irritating fashion.

He took a firm grip on his emotions and returned her greeting with a bland face. After yesterday's discovery of fondness for fools like Rod Mason he found he wasn't prepared to cut her even an inch of slack.

Carly tripped up the steps and asked

politely if she might have an hour off work in order to go into Jozini on urgent business.

Jason contrived to look coldly astonished. 'No, you may not, Miss Smith. You are employed to do a job of work here until four-thirty in the afternoon. Any personal business must be attended to in your own time.'

Carly bit her lip. If she left it until after work it might not give the police enough time to arrange things. It was vital that she wasted no further time.

'This is very urgent business,' she insisted. 'I really must have some time off.'

Jason folded his arms across his chest. 'No,' he told her implacably. 'Your urgent business will have to wait . . . unless perhaps your boyfriend is prepared to help? Perhaps he'd be only too willing to stand in for you here and undertake your dairy tasks while you're away?'

'My b-boyfriend?'

Jason's lip curled. 'The estimable

129

Rod Mason,' he drawled. 'I believe I saw you in his arms last night?'

Carly's cheeks turned bright red. 'Leave my personal life out of this,' she snapped. 'All I'm asking for is one hour off.'

'And the answer is no.'

Rod Mason was due to go into Jozini this afternoon to pick up a tractor tyre which they were having mended.

If Carly thought she could meet him there and waste work time dilly-dallying with her lover, she was very much mistaken!

Jasper, who had been listening intently, felt bound to intervene.

'Oh, surely, Jason . . . what harm can it do to give the lass an hour off? She's a good worker.'

A stony mask descended over Jason's features. 'With respect, Grandfather, I am in charge of the staff here. The granddaughter of Daniel MacDonald may be an excellent worker, but she may not have time off, and that is my final word.'

Jason almost dropped his stick. 'Daniel MacDonald? Did you say that Miss Smith is the granddaughter of Daniel MacDonald?' He turned to Carly, his blue eyes filled with indignation. 'Is this the truth?'

Carly drew herself up to her full height. 'Yes, it is, and I'd like to point out that my grandfather is the finest man I know. You two may have been at loggerheads for years, but that fact hardly concerns me or my work. All I ask is the right to do my job.'

'I'm exceedingly disappointed in you, Miss Smith,' Jasper retorted icily. 'Why did you not inform me of your connection to Daniel MacDonald when I offered you the position?'

'Why did you not ask?' Carly shot back.

Jasper's expression became every bit as stony as his grandson's.

'I'm afraid we have no option but to let you go, Miss Smith. Your contract will not be renewed after the month is up. Good day to you.'

Carly looked from one to the other, unable to believe what she was hearing. How could these people allow themselves to be so petty and prejudiced? She shook her head in sad disbelief. There was no way she was prepared to work for such small-minded, bigoted men.

'In that case,' she told them sweetly, 'I quit here and now. I shall have to begin looking for another job immediately, which will require me to take the odd hour off since I would have to attend interviews, and so on, and any such future requests would doubtless be refused.'

Jason hid his anger behind a cold mask. He would have liked to have shaken the girl. Why did she have to go and resign? With both her and Rod Mason gone by tomorrow, things at Kosi Park would fall into a sorry mess.

'Your cheque will be in the post.' He gritted. 'That will be all, Miss Smith.'

Carly had never been dismissed in such a cold, unreasonable manner before. It was highly insulting, but she had been brought up to be a lady. She would not descend to the level of turning the conversation into a slanging match. Neither was she prepared to beg.

'Thank you,' she said with quiet dignity. 'Goodbye, Mr Edwards . . . Mr Campbell.'

After collecting her belongings from the shed she flung them into the Mini and drove away from Kosi Park without a backward glance.

11

Half-an-hour later she was sitting in Detective Inspector Jeff Morgan's office in Jozini, pouring out her story. He thanked her gravely, walked her to her car and sketched a salute as she reversed out of the parking lot.

Mary MacDonald was sitting on the veranda with her knitting when Carly arrived back at Jozini Acres. She looked up in surprise.

'You're home early, dear.'

'Yes.

A closer look at her granddaughter's face caused her to ask quietly, 'is something wrong?'

A large tear rolled down Carly's cheek. 'I've packed in my job.'

Mary frowned. 'Oh? So soon? Would you like to tell me about it?'

For the second time in an hour Carly poured out her story. 'So you see, Gran,

I could hardly stay on at Kosi Park after that, could I?'

'No, you couldn't. Tell me, dear . . . what do you really think of Jason Edwards?'

Carly's mouth tightened. 'He's the most stubborn, trying man I know. At least, today he was . . . '

'Only today?'

Carly thought about yesterday, and how happy she'd been in his arms. 'Yesterday,' she sighed, 'he was a gorgeous hunk, and I could have sworn he fancied me.'

Mary hid a smile and picked up her knitting. All was not lost yet.

At six-thirty exactly, a small contingent of plain-clothes policemen arrived at Kosi Park, ostensibly as Jason's dinner guests.

Under cover of darkness he marched them down to Rod Mason's cottage where they concealed themselves behind the bushes.

By eight-fifteen Rod and his two accomplices had been apprehended and the firearms impounded.

As Jeff Morgan left, he turned to Jason. 'You weren't the only one who was on to our friend Mason, you know, Jason. I had an interesting visit from one of your employees this afternoon.'

'Oh? Which one?'

'A Miss Carly Smith.'

Jason's jaw dropped. 'You . . . you did?'

'Yes. She revealed that she'd been playing up to Mason in the interests of finding out more about his activities. Smart girl, that. She even pretended ignorance of the Zulu language so that she could eavesdrop on Mason and Chief Vuma's men, that's how she was able to find out about the impending faction fight.

'We'll be paying Chief Vuma a little visit tomorrow, to threaten him with the long arm of the law. Hopefully we'll have a little peace in the district for a while after this.'

He shook hands with Jason.

'Goodbye, old friend. Glad to have

you back in the area.'

Jason could not have spoken if he'd tried. He watched as the other man drove away, feeling the biggest jerk this side of the Zambezi. Like a fool he'd allowed his personal feelings to overcome his good judgement. As a result, he'd both misjudged and underestimated Miss Carly Smith . . . Big Time!

With a heavy heart he returned to the house to inform his grandfather about the night's proceedings and to file his final report for the Natal News. At least James O'Brien would not be able to say another word against the honourable Zululand farmer known as Jasper Campbell!

When he'd completed these tasks, Jason resolved to pour himself a stiff drink and take himself to bed.

Not that he'd be able to sleep.

12

News had travelled fast. There was much quiet consternation amongst the workers on both farms the following morning as they discussed the arrests.

They paid much more attention to their tasks and seemed relieved that the element of strife had been removed from their midst. The sullenness which had been present during the previous weeks had completely disappeared.

'I always said that man Mason was a bad fish,' Trifina told Nomsa, the scullery maid, 'always throwing his weight around and not doing any work himself.'

She glared at the towels as she stuffed them into the washing machine and added, 'Zondi tells me he saw the man trying to kiss Miss Carly on the path.'

Nomsa's brown eyes widened. 'Perhaps he wants to marry Miss Carly.'

'Oh, no, I wouldn't say that. Zondi said she wasn't looking very happy about it. He said Mr Mason wasn't at all pleased to see Mr Edwards arrive, and scooted off looking like somebody had knocked all the rungs out of his ladder.'

Trifina clicked her tongue in disgust. 'Miss Carly shall marry Mr Mason over my dead body! A jailbird is not the man for a lady like her. I should like to throw that Mr Mason over the cliff. He is a rogue.'

'He will have a hard time getting into heaven,' Nomsa agreed happily.

Jason, up to his eyeballs in supervising farming activities at Kosi Park, let it be known that a hard line would be taken with any similar offenders in the future. This announcement appeared to meet with great approval.

Most of the men and their families were patient, hard-working people who were only too pleased to be able to get on with their lives in peace.

By the end of the week's activities, Jason had to admit that he was hard-pressed to keep up. He found his new career hard but satisfying work, and realised that Kosi Park was too big an operation to be run without help from someone with more know-how.

At this point his thoughts turned to Carly; she knew exactly what she was about when it came to agriculture.

He still wasn't quite so sure she knew what she was about when it came to men, however. He hadn't ceased to think about her night and day. In his opinion she was the sweetest, most adorable, sassiest, most desirable woman around. And he very badly wanted to marry her.

Unfortunately it was Jason Edwards who had messed up, not Carly, he acknowledged ruefully. Still, where there was life there was hope. He was prepared to eat any amount of humble pie should Carly be prepared to listen.

Not a man to be daunted by one

misunderstanding, Jason was determined to get what he wanted, and that was to be able to settle down in peace with the woman he loved.

An idea had been tumbling about in his head all day. Tomorrow, Saturday, he intended to implement it. All it would take was one telephone call this evening to Mary MacDonald . . .

After breakfast the following morning he said casually, 'I'd like to take you for a drive in the new Merc, Grandfather, so you can see how well she handles. Will you come? We'll have a jaunt around the district and then go into Jozini for lunch. We could take in a movie afterwards, if you like. What do you say?'

Jasper folded his table napkin and placed it in its silver holder. A little outing would be very nice.

'Sounds fine to me, Jason.'

Secretly, he was rather pleased. Jason had been working hard all week and needed some form of relaxation. The boy had been a little down in the mouth, too. Perhaps the responsibility of keeping Kosi Park going was too much? Hopefully the lad would soon find his feet, because if he decided to throw in the towel and go back to journalism, he didn't think his old heart would be able to stand it.

Jason seated his grandfather solicitously in the passenger seat and placed his walking stick in the back. He climbed into the Mercedes and reversed from the garage with his heart in his mouth. Supposing his plan failed?

'Nice morning,' he observed casually as the car purred down the drive.

'It certainly is,' Jasper agreed.

Privately, Jasper hoped his grandfather would still think so by lunchtime!

The Mercedes cruised around the country roads to its heart's content while Jasper reminisced happily about the places he'd been to and the people he'd known and his grandson patiently listened. When Jason approached the gateposts of Jozini

Acres, the old man fell silent.

'What the dickens are you doing?'

Jason had turned into the driveway and was proceeding at a sedate pace towards the homestead.

'I have some business with the MacDonalds, Grandfather,' Jason told him calmly.

Jasper paled. 'In that case, I have no option but to remain in the car until you are finished.'

'Oh, no, Grandfather, Mary Mac-Donald specifically said I was to bring you inside for morning tea. She is expecting us both; you're surely too much of a gentleman to disappoint her?'

Jasper huffed. 'You arranged this, didn't you?'

Jason pretended not to hear. He climbed out of the car and went around to the passenger side to assist the old man, helping him slowly up the veranda steps.

Mary was waiting at the door with a bright smile on her face.

'How delightful to see you again, Jasper,' she greeted him warmly, 'welcome to Jozini Acres. Do come into the living-room.'

Unable to speak, Jasper accompanied her down the passage. He'd expected the wife of his old enemy to hate him; after all, he and Daniel had clashed many times.

Once her guests were seated, Mary rang for Trifina to bring in the tea tray and chattered about the subject closest to her heart; her garden.

'Lovely weather we're having. My spring bulbs are just about over, but the annuals are starting now, thankfully.'

She smiled at Jasper, determined to dispel any awkwardness. Mary, who knew all there was to know about roses, was then gracious enough to ask Jasper for his advice. She listened intently as he gave it, albeit stiffly.

Trifina beamed when she saw who the visitors were. She greeted them politely and withdrew to the kitchen with many happy mutterings about a bright future for Miss Carly, so that Nomsa, who was busy with the dishes, was emboldened to suggest that the housekeeper start saving for a new outfit to wear to the wedding.

'Pink,' Trifina concurred with satisfaction. 'I have always fancied myself in pink. Naturally we shall invite the whole district . . . '

Jason accepted his cup of tea from Mary and smiled. She was wonderful at keeping the conversation ball rolling.

'How are things on the farm?' he asked in a conversational tone.

Mary took up the hint and chatted animatedly about the healthy state of Daniel's herds, enthusing animatedly about the newest bull calf.

'He is expected for tea in a moment,' she added.

'Who, the calf?' Jason quipped.

She laughed. 'No, Daniel.'

'Who's taking my name in vain?' her husband enquired jovially as he entered the living-room. He gazed at the visitors, stood riveted to the carpet and paled. He turned to Mary and demanded, 'Jasper Campbell? In my living-room?'

'I invited them for tea,' she told him firmly as she poured another cup. 'Sit down, Daniel, dear. It appears that Jasper's grandson has something to say to us all.'

Pride dictated that Daniel remember his manners. He shook hands reluctantly with both Jasper and Jason, and stalked to his seat.

'Say it quickly, then, lad. I have work to do,' he growled.

'You don't usually work on a Saturday morning,' his wife corrected sweetly. 'You and Carly make a point of relaxing then, after your busy week, don't you?'

Daniel looked thunderous. 'Where is the girl?'

'She'll be here in a moment. I sent her to collect some more eggs. Jason dear,' she begged, 'do go and find her; she's out at the back. Would you ask her to come in for tea, now, please?'

Jason was only too happy to comply.

He walked through the kitchen where Trifina and her sidekick greeted him happily before rushing to the window where they proceeded to watch with interest as he went into the garden.

13

Carly was walking up the path from the henhouse with her basket of eggs. She was wearing an old blue cotton dress and her hair fell in a glorious golden curtain down her back. Jason thought she had never looked more beautiful.

'Hello, Carly.'

She looked up in amazement at the sound of his voice. A heavy frown descended as her brown eyes snapped with anger. Of all the cheek, putting his feet back on her own turf!

'What are you doing here?' she demanded rudely.

'Mary sent me to find you. I've brought my grandfather to visit you and we're all waiting for you in the living-room.'

Carly's mouth fell open. 'Holy Moly. That should be some party. I don't understand why . . . '

'No, but you soon will.'

Much to the watching Trifina's satisfaction he leant down and kissed her on the cheek. 'I owe you an apology, Carly.'

She gazed up at him suspiciously. 'Oh?' Her tone wasn't very encouraging.

Jasper took a deep breath. 'I know all about your so-called relationship with Rod Mason, and why.'

'I see.'

'I suppose you know he was successfully arrested?'

'Who doesn't? The labourers have talked about nothing else all week.'

'Am I forgiven?'

Carly wanted it in black and white. 'What for, exactly?'

Jason's face was wiped of all expression, but his eyes on hers were intent. Carly had the distinct impression that he was nervous.

'For misjudging you so badly. Am I forgiven?'

She pursed her lips. 'Well, yes . . . I

suppose so. After all, what is the little matter of being sacked from one's job because of unfounded prejudice? Unfair dismissal, I think they call it.'

A dull tide of red arose beneath Jason's collar. 'That would be an accurate description.'

He took her by the arm. 'Your Grandmother is waiting . . .'

Carly preceded him into the living-room and glanced at the silent company with interest. What was going on here?

Jason cleared his throat. He didn't believe in beating around the bush.

'I've arranged this meeting this morning in order to clarify a few things,' he began. 'Firstly, I should like to make my future intentions known. Carly doesn't know it yet, but I love her and I intend to ask her to marry me.'

Carly's gasp was loud in the ensuing silence. Jason gave her a tender smile. 'I fell in love with you from the first moment I saw you, and when you are quite ready, I will ask you properly.'

'Now look here . . .' began Daniel.

Jason held up his hand. 'May I continue?'

'Hrrmph.'

'Your granddaughter, sir, is feisty, independent and determined; qualities she has no doubt inherited from you. With Carly at my side I would very much like to continue farming at Kosi Park, and will be offering her the position of farm manager. Should she feel that she is able to accept, Jason Edwards will be greatly relieved. I need her expertise, hard work and enthusiasm.'

'But Jason,' Jasper growled when he had recovered his breath, 'have you taken leave of your senses? She's a MacDonald!'

'And that is precisely why I have arranged this meeting. I mean no disrespect to you two old men,' Jason told them firmly, 'but isn't it about time you dispensed with these senseless hostilities? Think about it. When Carly and I marry we'll all be related.

'When our children arrive, do not

think for one moment that we would be prepared to put up with constant strife and disharmony between their great grandparents, who, remember, are the only relatives they'd have.

'We would rather have no family ties at all than ones which continue to lacerate our emotions and that of our children. If necessary we would leave the district and move away in order to make a life for ourselves elsewhere.'

He paused. 'Do I make myself clear?'

There was a stunned silence.

All at once Carly found her voice. 'I agree with Jason,' she said quietly. 'Should we marry I want no part in a destructive lifestyle, either. I want to live in a family where there's peace and harmony. The opposite of bitterness and strife,' she pointed out, 'is love and forgiveness. I hope we can all see our way clear to becoming reconciled.'

Daniel took a deep, shuddering breath. Talk about a brave laddie!

'Much as it pains me to admit it, Jason, you are quite right. I appreciate what you have said.' He added slowly, 'I for one would not like to see my granddaughter living at the other end of the country simply because I proved to be a stubborn, unforgiving old man. I want to be a part of her life. I want to be part of the lives of my great-grandchildren.'

He turned to his old enemy. 'What do you say, Jasper?'

Jasper's eyes were unexpectedly moist.

'I say there is no fool like an old one,' he said unsteadily. 'We've both been old fools, Daniel. It has taken my grandson to show us today just how foolish we've been.'

He took out his handkerchief and blew his nose. 'Carly Smith, you are a grand little lass. Should you accept my grandson's proposal of marriage, it would make one old man very happy.'

He turned to Daniel. 'We're too old to continue with this nonsense, my old friend. Feuding clans are not for this day and age; we should know better. I'm tired of having to keep up hostilities, I find it sours the mind. I say we stop being at loggerheads and bury the past.' His voice roughened. 'I've already lost a wife and only daughter. Why should I allow pride to lose me my grandson, too?'

'I was hoping you'd say that, Jasper. We'll let bygones be bygones.'

Daniel rose stiffly from his chair and extended a work-roughened hand. 'Shall we shake on it?'

As the two old men sealed their pact with grave faces, Mary surreptitiously wiped her eyes on her lace handkerchief.

'This calls for more tea,' she said briskly, and reached for the small, silver bell at her side.

14

Under cover of the continuing conversation Carly went up to Jason. 'Did you mean all that? I can have my job back?'

'I meant it, Carly. You will find that I'm a man of my word. You can have your job back with promotion.'

She pretended to think. 'You'll allow me free rein with the beef cattle and an absolute say when it comes to the dairy herd?'

'They're all yours.'

'I also need to take charge of the silage,' she informed him firmly.

'Silage . . . ?'

At his look of incomprehension, she explained. 'The feed for the cattle. It has to be made just right, you see. The key to making it is lush grass and a couple of days of hot, sunny weather. Wet weather can delay the whole process.'

Jason tried to look intelligent. 'It can?'

'Sure. We have to mow the grass, spread it with a grass turner and leave the sun to draw out the moisture so it's easier to transport. If it rained some of the important sugars in the grass would be washed out.'

'Oh, really?'

'There's not a lot of time to waste. We must try to make it by the end of November,' she urged, 'then it must be covered in plastic sheeting weighed down with some of those old tractor tyres I saw in the shed. The grass must be left to pickle in its own juice, you see.'

'Sounds fascinating,' he murmured.

Encouraged by Jason's apparent interest, Carly enlarged upon the theme. 'You have to understand that it's crucial to boost the food value so that the cows are in fine fettle for mating. They must be given the best possible chance for conceiving if we're to improve the dairy herd.'

Jason's mouth twitched. 'Right.'

When she launched into the possibility of artificial insemination using Aberdeen Angus bulls, and looked set to improve his education further, Jason cut her lovingly short.

'Like I said, Carly, it's all yours. You can do what you like.'

'Well . . . it's an offer I can hardly refuse, really. Since you are being so generous, Jason, I feel I must accept.'

'There's just one condition.'

'And that is . . . ?'

'That you think about us.'

For the moment she looked blank. 'What about us?'

Jason spelled it out. 'I would like a future with you, Carly. Anything else for me would be totally unthinkable.'

Carly gazed up at him, her brown eyes warmly humorous. 'I can see that you're a man who knows exactly what he wants and is fearless in his attempts to achieve it.'

'Spot on. I've lived too long with the cares of the world on my shoulders,

Carly. Running about the globe reporting day in and day out on crime, wars, famine and strife has left me sickened. All I want now is to live out my life in peace and fulfilment with the woman I love.'

He paused. 'I want us to remain at Kosi Park and rebuild it into the success it once was. In time, and with your grandfather's permission, we might even combine operations with Jozini Acres so that our children will have a decent inheritance. But most of all, Carly, I want us to grow old together. I'll give you all the time in the world to decide, and when you've done so, I'll be waiting to receive your answer.'

Carly reached up and put her arms about his neck.

'At the risk of being thought the brazen hussy you imagined me to be the other day, Jason, I'd like you to kiss me,' she commanded. 'And make sure you do a good job while you're at it.'

Jason's grey eyes had darkened to pewter, a sure sign of deep emotion.

'I won't keep you waiting for your answer, Jason. I'll marry you whenever you like. A career is all very well, but not at the expense of love. And here I'm being offered both. I'm a very lucky girl.'

Jason's heartbeat went into overdrive. 'Now you're talking.'

She added thoughtfully, 'anything else for me, to, would be unthinkable. How could I work day after day at Kosi Park and hide my love for you? I'm the kind of person who doesn't do things by half measures, so I'm jumping in with both feet. I'll try my best to be a good farmer, a good wife, and when the time comes, a good mother as well.'

Jason could scarcely contain his joy. 'Then we too, will seal our pact.' He drew her into his arms and murmured, 'so much nicer to love than to hate. We'd better do this often, just to remind ourselves.'

★　★　★

159

As his mouth covered hers Carly heard the applause of her grandfather and his new-found friend in the background.

'Ay, that's the way, lad,' Jasper was saying proudly, 'that's the way!'

Daniel, not to be outdone, put his arms around Mary's shoulders.

'Your grandmother will help you with the little girls, Carly, and I'll be teaching the boys how to fish . . . '

When she had breath, Jason's bride gazed up at him and giggled. 'What have we started, Jason?'

Unperturbed, he took his time about kissing her again.

'Whatever it is, sweetheart,' he said firmly when he'd made a good job of it, 'we'll make sure it has no ending.'

THE END

We do hope that you have enjoyed reading this large print book.

Did you know that all of our titles are available for purchase?

We publish a wide range of high quality large print books including:
Romances, Mysteries, Classics
General Fiction
Non Fiction and Westerns

Special interest titles available in large print are:
The Little Oxford Dictionary
Music Book, Song Book
Hymn Book, Service Book

Also available from us courtesy of Oxford University Press:
Young Readers' Dictionary
(large print edition)
Young Readers' Thesaurus
(large print edition)

For further information or a free brochure, please contact us at:
Ulverscroft Large Print Books Ltd.,
The Green, Bradgate Road, Anstey,
Leicester, LE7 7FU, England.
Tel: (00 44) 0116 236 4325
Fax: (00 44) 0116 234 0205

REBECCA'S REVENGE

Valerie Holmes

Rebecca Hind's life is thrown into turmoil when her brother mysteriously disappears and she cannot keep up rent payments for their humble cottage. Help is offered by Mr Paignton of Gorebeck Lodge, although Rebecca is reluctant to leave with him and his mysterious companion. However, faced with little choice and determined to survive, Rebecca takes the offered position at the Lodge — and enters a strange world where she finds hate and love living side by side . . .